DREADFUL SUMMIT

STANLEY
ELLIN

Introduction by
ANDREW
KLAVAN

AMERICAN
MYSTERY
CLASSICS

Penzler Publishers
New York

Published in 2026 by Penzler Publishers
58 Warren Street, New York, NY 10007
penzlerpublishers.com

Distributed by Simon & Schuster

Cover image: Andy Ross
Cover design: Mauricio Diaz

Paperback ISBN 978-1-61316-769-4
Hardcover ISBN 978-1-61316-768-7

Library of Congress Control Number: 2025950448

Printed in the United States of America

9 8 7 6 5 4 3 2 1

OTTO PENZLER PRESENTS
AMERICAN MYSTERY CLASSICS

DREADFUL SUMMIT

Stanley Ellin (1916–1986) was an American mystery writer born in Brooklyn, New York. His first short story, titled "The Specialty of the House" appeared in 1948 in Ellery Queen's Mystery Magazine. He was a three-time winner of the Edgar Allen Poe Award, for his short stories "The House Party" in 1954 and "The Blessington Method" in 1956, and for his novel *The Eighth Circle* in 1959. His novels *Dreadful Summit*, *House of Cards*, and *The Bind* were each adapted into feature films. A longtime member of the Mystery Writers of America, Ellin was awarded the group's Grand Master Award in 1981.

Andrew Klavan is the *New York Times* bestselling author of numerous crime novels including *True Crime*, filmed by Clint Eastwood; *Don't Say A Word*, filmed starring Michael Douglas; and the Cameron Winter series. He has been nominated for the Edgar Award six times and has won twice. Aside from penning bestselling fiction and nonfiction and screenplays to blockbuster films, Klavan's political satire videos have been viewed by tens of millions of people, and he currently hosts *The Andrew Klavan Show* at The Daily Wire.

INTRODUCTION

"I think I liked Al Judge a lot before I knew I had to kill him."

THERE ARE novels that live past their moment and novels that simply don't, and you can usually tell which kind you're reading within the first few sentences. Read the opening lines of Stanley Ellin's *Dreadful Summit* and you will instantly recognize a vital voice, just as startling and electric today as it was in 1948, the year the book was published. It is the voice of a boy on the brink of manhood, a voice full of pridefulness and violence and burbling sexuality. A voice that anyone who has been a boy or known a boy will recognize and understand. It grips you on page one and does not let go until the story is finished.

This sort of durable vitality is not a common thing in

any kind of novel, but it is even more unusual in genre fiction. Good genre novels don't always excel as literature because they can fulfill the requirements of their genre—mystery, thrills, horror, sci-fi futurism—without providing the kind of depth and insight and emotional complexity that keeps a book vibrant decades after it's written. But when the quality is there, nothing could be better. An exciting story brimming over with humanity—that's what we readers are here for. That's what you'll find in *Dreadful Summit.*

If you thrill to this living voice and think to yourself, "Wait, who is this writer?" or "How did I never hear of Stanley Ellin before?" you won't be alone. When Ellin died in 1986, the headline of his obituary in the *Los Angeles Time*s was "Award Winner's Works Better Known Than Name."

It was that way for me certainly. I first encountered Ellin's writing when I was a boy in sleepaway summer camp in the 1960's. Our counselor, like all good male camp counselors, took upon himself the responsibility of scaring the bejabbers out of his young charges just at bedtime. He didn't want us to miss the essential camp experience of stifling our terrified sobs in our pillows throughout our first sleepless night. Being a young man of literary pretensions, the counselor did not simply make up some cheap spook story about the boy who drowned in the lake outside and whose hungry ghost was just waiting for us to go swimming there tomorrow. He saved that for the second night. That first night, he read us a short story called, "The Specialty of the House." I will not give the story away because you should read it yourself. But I will say this. It may be the eeriest work of American short fiction since Edgar Allan Poe's "The Cask of Amontillado," to which it bears some resemblance.

Along with *Dreadful Summit*, "The Specialty of the House," published the same year in *Ellery Queen Mystery Magazine,* marked Ellin's debut as a writer. Before that, he had supported his wife and daughter doing the sort of eclectic work with which many struggling writers are familiar. He was a boilermaker's apprentice, a steel worker, a dairy farmer and a teacher plus he also served in the US Army during the final year of World War II. But once he began publishing, his works were rapidly snapped up by Hollywood to feed the hungry maws of 1950s and '60s television anthology series like *Suspense, Westinghouse Desilu Playhouse,* and, most frequently, *Alfred Hitchcock Presents.*

It was through Hitchcock's wonderful show that I continued to enjoy Ellin's work without learning his name. To enhance the spookiness of the Hitchcock experience, I and sometimes a pal would make a tent in my bedroom with a blanket thrown over some chairs. We'd then wheel my black-and-white TV under the canopy. And there, with the room dark around us, we would gleefully shiver to the murderous ironies of such Ellin tales as "Help Wanted," about a husband who tries to pay for his wife's operation by becoming a hit man, "The Blessington Method," about a very disturbing way to avoid the burden of elderly relatives, and, of course, "The Specialty of the House," which was almost as eerie on TV as it was on the page.

It was as a short story writer that Ellin thrived, though his writing method was so slow and meticulous he averaged only a little more than one story a year. Of his three Edgar Allan Poe Awards from the Mystery Writers of America, two were for his short stories. Four other Ellin stories were nominated for the prize.

But he also won an Edgar for his 1959 novel *The Eighth Circle*. And in 1981, he received the MWA's highest honor, the Grand Master Award. Because, while short stories were Ellin's chief metier, he could handle the long form with expertise, as *Dreadful Summit* proves beyond a doubt.

The novel takes place in a single twenty-four-hour period, but in that compressed timeframe, it captures the painful essence of a boy's journey into manhood. Its narrator is George LaMain, the bookish teenaged son of a New York bar owner. LaMain is forced to look on helplessly when the father he idolizes is publicly humiliated by a well-connected sportswriter. It's an excruciating scene. We live it along with George. We feel his adolescent illusions shattering like glass. And we have no trouble understanding and sympathizing with his night-long mission of revenge against the sportswriter, the only path he sees into manhood.

What starts out as a simple there-and-back adventure soon becomes a wandering odyssey of frustration, humiliation, desire and confrontation—all the experiences of growing up male packed into a single night and day. What is remarkable is the way Ellin simultaneously tightens two parallel lines of suspense. One, the exterior line, is built on George's headlong plunge toward an act of violence that will surely destroy his life. The other, the interior line, is the emotional tension of a boy striving to become the man he thought his father was.

After you read the book, it's fascinating to watch *The Big Night,* the film noir adaptation that was made three years after the novel's publication. Despite the title, it's a small picture, only an hour and fifteen minutes long, but there's impressive talent behind it. Ellin co-wrote the screenplay with the director Joseph Losey, and with assists from the Oscar-winning screenwriter Ring

Lardner Jr. and the Oscar-nominated Hugo Butler. Losey himself was a high-end, award-winning director, who would go on to make *The Servant* and *The Go-Between*, both scripted by Harold Pinter. Young George is played by John Drew Barrymore, a scion of the famous acting clan, and the father of the actress Drew Barrymore. This was his debut role.

With all that talent on hand, it's not surprising that the film captures some of the kinetic energy and grit of the novel. It even visualizes the scene from the book in which George rehearses his hoped-for vengeance by waving a gun and issuing threats at a mirror. Film buffs will immediately recognize the prototype of Robert DeNiro's more famous scene in Martin Scorsese's *Taxi Driver*. The resemblance may be coincidental, but the underlying inspiration is certainly the same: a young man coming to grips with the age-old connection between masculine identity and violence.

Still, as the film goes on, Hollywood censorship and 1950's cinematic delicacy strip the original story of its frank sexuality and hardboiled conclusions. The film is good, but it only serves to underscore just how very, very much better the source novel is.

For me, reading *Dreadful Summit* was like bumping into an old friend I didn't know I had. Two paragraphs in, I was swept up in a narrative by a writer I thought was a stranger, only to find I had known and loved his work since I was a boy lying fearfully awake at summer camp. But, if in fact, you have never experienced a Stanley Ellin story before, then congratulations. You are about to encounter the work—and learn the name—of one of the masters of the craft.

—Andrew Klavan

DREADFUL SUMMIT

HAMLET: *It waves me forth again; I'll follow it.*

HORATIO: *What if it tempt you toward the flood, my lord.*
Or to the dreadful summit of the cliff . . .

CHAPTER ONE

I NEVER saw Al Judge before that night.

On the top of his column in the *Daily Press* they had a picture of him, but it wasn't a very good picture. In the picture he had wavy black hair and kind of a thin, pointed face, but when I saw him his hair was almost all gray, and his face was soft and pudgy. There was a big roll of fat under his chin, and his eyes were squinted up under more fat. I guess it was a pretty old picture.

I used to read the *Press* every night before I went to bed. I started with the pictures, and plenty of times they showed nice-looking girls with lots of stuff showing, or maybe wrecks with bodies laying around. That was all right.

Then I read all the comics, even the ones I didn't like so much. They had two pages of comics, and I started at the top of the left-hand page and read all the way down, and then I did the same thing with the right-hand page. It felt wrong if I didn't read them before I went to bed. Like one night, Buttsy, the newspaper boy, didn't leave any papers. He used to leave some at the bar every night, and then have a free beer. The night he didn't leave them, I went out and bought the *Press* because I couldn't go to sleep until I read the comics.

After that I would read down page three, which is the page with all the killings and stuff. Nearly every night there would be something about a husband catching his wife naked with another man, or some crazy guy grabbing a little girl and giving her the works. When I went to bed I would try and see the whole thing happening in my mind.

Mostly I didn't read other news, because it had numbers in it. I mean, stuff about Democrats or Republicans or Russia and it would be all full of big numbers. That stuff puts me to sleep.

The part I saved for last was the sports section. And the best thing in it was Al Judge's column, "The Judge's Bench." It was a good column all right, all about the different sports and about people who hung around sports. Sometimes in his column he would write about an Irishman or an Italian or a Jew he knew about, and then he would kid them along and write in their kind of dialect. I had to laugh when I read it.

Every Saturday in the column he would call it "Judge's Decisions," and he would tell inside stuff about tinhorn gamblers and how they were dirtying up sports. He put their names right down, and he wasn't afraid of anyone. I think I liked Al Judge a lot before I knew I had to kill him.

That night was November eighth, and I know because it was my sixteenth birthday, and I was sitting in back of the bar waiting to go to the fights at Madison Square Garden with my father. My father's name is Andy LaMain, and he owned Handy Andy's Bar and Grill near Ninth Avenue and Twentieth Street.

Once it used to be just plain Andy's Bar and Grill. Then Flanagan, the helper, told me a guy one time asked, "What kind of a name is LaMain?" and my father said, "French."

"Well, what does it mean in French?"

My father said, "It means 'the hand,'" and that's how they got to calling him Handy Andy. He liked it, so he put it on the window. It's better than what the kids call me over at High School. They call me Froggy because my father was French, and they think it's a big joke because I'm not even the oldest one in the class but I'm big and I look older than anybody.

Sometimes I come into a new class and everybody shuts up because they think maybe I'm the teacher. Then they see where I sit so they know I'm not, and they start picking on me and making all kinds of jokes about it. Even the teachers pick on me because they must figure I'm older than anybody around, only they call me by my real name. My real name is George LaMain after my grandfather, but he spelled it Georges with an *s* because he came from France and that's how they do it there.

My grandfather was a hero all right. He didn't have to, but when the First World War started, he went back to France so he could get in the army there, and he got killed in the Battle of Verdun. I have his picture, and he is standing there in his uniform looking pretty tough. My father said that my grandfather was never afraid of anything. Plenty of times I think that when the next war comes I will be built up so I can put on a uniform and maybe die a hero like my grandfather.

I think I could have even got into the Marines in this war if I wanted to. Plenty of times I read in the *Press* about kids only fourteen, fifteen, who got in and nobody guessed how old they were until their mothers started yelling or something. That wouldn't have stopped me because I didn't have any mother to worry about. Long ago my father told me how she died when I was only a little kid.

Anyhow, the way I look, I think I could have got into the Marines easy if they didn't mind me being a little skinny. Only when my father read about one of the kids once, he made a crack about it so I knew he wouldn't like it. He wanted me around the bar where he could see I didn't get into any trouble.

The Bar and Grill is long and very narrow, and as soon as you step in from the street you are standing at the bar. It is so narrow that if a couple of guys bunch up at the bar, you have to squeeze by them to get to the back. In the back is a cookstove against the wall, and some old tables and chairs. Flanagan, the helper, could cook good hamburgers on that stove. Thick, kind of raw, with raw onions on top. He made good frankfurters too. Suppertimes he would make me mostly chops and beans because that's where I ate supper.

I was just finishing supper when Al Judge came in. I had steak and French fried potatoes because it was my birthday, and I was drinking coke out of a bottle because my father wouldn't let me drink beer or any hard stuff. That was all right with me because I didn't really like beer anyhow. One time, when my father wasn't there, Flanagan let me try a little but it tasted awful. I figured it would be like the nut-brown ale Robin Hood used to drink, because I read about it and I knew beer was a lot like ale. But when I imagined drinking nut-brown ale, it always tasted like root beer, which is a good drink.

Flanagan was scared after he let me try the beer, because he knew how my father felt. My father wouldn't let me smoke either, or talk about girls. He was very strict.

But for my birthday he promised he would take Frances and me to the fights at the Garden. Frances was his girl friend. Her name was Frances Sedziaski, but she was awfully pretty, not big like some Polacks are. Only she used to nag me about church and eating and that kind of stuff. I guess she couldn't help it, because she was a nurse over at Chelsea Hospital, so what with feeding the sick people and watching the priest send them off when they died, she was a bug on those angles.

One time she said, "You don't eat enough, and you read too much. My God, you're only a kid, and you look like an old man." And then when she could she would cook supper for me upstairs in our rooms. All lettuce and tomatoes and stuff.

Sometimes we were walking together and the guys would give her the eye—she was blonde and she even looked good in her nurse's uniform—and then she would turn red and say to me, "See that? Do you want to grow up like that? When was the last time you went to confession?" Just as if *I* did something!

So I lied about it and told her a week ago, two weeks ago, or I promised to go pretty soon. She knew I was lying about it, but she couldn't say so.

I say one thing for her though. She was crazy about my father. Every day, she called up at the bar at least once, and when they both had free time together, she was always around. Now and then he gave me money to carry me over a weekend, and he would take a trip somewhere. I figured Frances was with him, but it wasn't any of my business. Anyhow, I liked eating by myself. I could eat for two hours and almost read a whole book.

When my father first told me Frances was coming along to the fights, I didn't like the idea too much. Rocks Abruzzo was fighting Joe Shotfield, and Rocks is a real killer. Biff bam! He socks them and they stay down.

But if Frances was there and saw too much blood or something, she might say how awful it was and even want to go home. So when my father told me that Frances wasn't coming, a couple of weeks later, it was all right with me.

Now and then Frances and my father would have real loud arguments, and she wouldn't show up for a couple of days. This time she wasn't around for more than a week, and I figured they must have had a real bust-up. It couldn't have happened at a better time.

I didn't mind eating supper at a back table of the bar, because I could read while I was eating. I was reading a book called *Kim* by Rudyard Kipling. I didn't like it at the beginning, but it got better as you went along. It was about a boy in India who was a spy. He wasn't afraid of anything, and he was plenty smart. I kept the book under the bar, and I read some of it every night at supper.

I was so busy reading that I didn't hear Al Judge come in. Or the others either. Then everything got so quiet that I looked up. A lot of quiet can be just as noisy as a lot of noise, if you get what I mean. Like when they tore down the Ninth Avenue "L" and I couldn't fall asleep at night because the trains weren't banging along any more by my window.

So I looked up, and then I saw this man standing at the bar. He was a big man with gray wavy hair and that kind of fattish face I told you about. He had on a big black overcoat with the buttons all open, and around his neck he had a long white scarf that hung down loose in front of him. And he had a cane in his hand.

Standing right alongside him was Sam Schwartz who is a delivery driver for the *Press* and plenty tough.

He curses like anything when the candy-store man takes too long counting out money on collection day, only now he wasn't saying anything. Just standing there and looking at my father. And standing with his back to the door was another delivery-man with a twisted nose whom I didn't know. I knew he was a delivery driver because he had his work apron on with the words "Daily Press" printed on it in big red letters. There were six or seven regular customers standing at the bar and drinking, and they all stopped talking. It was so quiet my ears hummed.

The big man with the cane hardly opened his mouth when he talked so it was hard to hear him. He said to my father, "You're LaMain, aren't you?" and my father said, "Yes, Mr. Judge."

That's how I knew it was Al Judge, because it wasn't a usual kind of name, and he looked a little like his picture too. He said, "You know why I'm here, don't you, LaMain?"

I never saw my father scared about anything in my whole life, but I knew from the way his face went all pale and sick that he was now. All he did was nod his head up and down while everybody looked at him, not saying a word.

Then Al Judge walked up to the clear space where the bar ended, and I saw why he carried a cane. He was lame in one leg; not much, but enough so he rocked a little when he walked. He pointed the cane at my father and said, "Come out here, LaMain."

My father looked at the guys standing behind the bar, but they just looked back at him. He ran a hand over his forehead, and even from where I was I could see his hand shaking. Then he turned to look at me, and he wasn't like my father at all. Once he used to know how everything should be done, and he wasn't afraid of anything, but now he was just standing there and shaking.

I started to get up, but Sam Schwartz pointed his finger at me and Flanagan grabbed my shoulders and pushed me down into the chair again. In my heart I was just as glad. Maybe I could have grabbed up the bottle and gotten in one lick before I went down. Maybe I could have broken off the neck of the bottle and shoved the sharp part into Al Judge's face before he or Sam Schwartz got to me, but I didn't really want to. I don't like fights or getting hurt. I try to talk my way out, and if I can't, I'm a good runner. I'm skinny but I'm tall and I can run.

So I wanted to do something, but I didn't want to, and inside of me I could feel I was getting ready to vomit. I locked it back and all that came up was a big belch, and a taste of coke in my mouth. But nobody thought it was funny. Nobody even looked at me.

And all this time Al Judge kept his cane pointed right at my father, and then, very slowly, my father walked down to the end of the bar, and came out, and stood in front of him. Al Judge put the cane down and leaned on it.

"Take off your shirt, LaMain," he said. "I want to see some skin."

"Before God, Mr. Judge!" my father started to say, but Al Judge just laughed short and sharp like a seal barking.

"Before me," he said.

My father looked at him and there were tears in his eyes. Then all of a sudden they started spilling out of mine and my glasses misted right over so that everything was blurred. I didn't even try to clean them. Only through the fog I could see my father slip the apron loop over his head, then take off his shirt. There was a big hole in the chest of his underwear and he held the shirt in front so it wouldn't show. Al Judge shook his head. "I said *skin.*"

My father folded up the shirt carefully and put it on the bar. Then he pulled off the underwear top and stood there with his skin all sweaty in the light.

"Get on your hands and knees, LaMain," said Al Judge. "Let's get it over with."

Outside the plate glass in front, I could see a lot of people pushing and shoving at each other. Some even pushed at the door, but the delivery-man I didn't know just snapped the lock and stood there like everybody else, stone quiet.

And then Al Judge lifted the cane and my father yelled so that it felt like a needle in my eardrums. I shut my eyes quick, and I knew I was ready to go out cold. Flanagan must have known too. He shoved my head so hard down on the table that my nose twisted under me and my whole face pained. But it couldn't drown out the slam of that cane and my father's voice bubbling out from him.

I was out all right. Because the next thing I heard was a whirling roar of noise that steadied down to a bunch of people all pushing around my father who was laid out on his belly on the floor with his head pushing up against the bar.

Flanagan was next to him on his knees. He had a bottle of whisky open and he was pouring it all over my father's back, and my father was alive all right because he was groaning.

The funniest thing was when I could sit up straight and the whole room stopped rocking around, I thought it was a dream. I mean, my father must have come out from behind the bar and slipped on a wet spot, or maybe somebody took a sneak punch at him like had happened once before. But he couldn't have been down on his knees with Al Judge caning him.

He couldn't, you see.

But when I felt how my glasses were all twisted where my head was shoved down on the table, and my nose hurt, and my neck, from Flanagan's hand, I understood all the way through me it was real.

Then I knew I had to kill Al Judge.

CHAPTER TWO

I'LL SAY this much for Flanagan. He wasn't much to look at, but he was a handy man to have around in a pinch. He was so old he didn't have much hair left, only a sort of dirty-white horseshoe around the top of his head. And instead of real teeth, he had a set of false ones, top and bottom, and when he got excited and started talking too fast they would come loose and start rattling around his mouth and he would have to shove them back with his finger.

On account of that, all the steadies liked to get him riled up so that his teeth would start slipping loose and then they would have a good laugh. He was easy to get riled up too, about almost everything. Especially wom-en. He would start yelling about how women made all the trouble in the world, with his teeth hopping around in his mouth until he nearly swallowed them and all the customers would die laughing. Then he would shove the teeth back in place and take a *True Story* magazine into the toilet and sit there until he cooled off.

He always meant to write the story of his life for *True Story* magazine, because he said people would really learn something if they read it, but he never got around to it. Sometimes he got around to taking a pencil and starting off on a piece of paper, but he never got past writing "The Story of My Life," and then somebody would come in for a beer or a rye or something and he would have to go back to work. I guess he never did get around to it.

Nobody ever called him anything except Flanagan. He worked for my father from as far back as I can remember, but he wouldn't ever tell his first name. Even to my father. When my father made out government papers for Flanagan, like taxes or something, he just put down X. Flanagan. It never bothered my father any. He said every man is entitled to one secret anyhow.

Flanagan used to worry about me an awful lot when I was a kid, and it was his idea I ought to go down and join the C.Y.O. because all I did was hang around the back of the bar after school and read books. I read almost everything by Rudyard Kipling and Alexandre

Dumas and good books like that, and I read all the comic books I could get and picture magazines. After a while I had to wear glasses from reading so much.

Flanagan worried about this and he took me to the C.Y.O. which is the Catholic Youth Organization on Seventeenth Street because they had sports and fresh air. But I couldn't see too good, and the kids didn't like me. I was always last pick on the teams, and I made believe I didn't care but finally I quit going.

Then Flanagan saw a sign in the subway that said how good the Boy Scouts were, and he took me down to the public-school basement and I joined the Boy Scouts. But the same thing happened at the Boy Scouts that happened at the C.Y.O., and besides I felt funny in the uniform because I was way taller than the other kids. The best thing they had was the *Boy Scout Handbook* which has plenty to read in it and a lot of pictures. I read it all through, and when I quit the Boy Scouts I kept the *Handbook*. I still like to read it.

After I quit the Boy Scouts, Flanagan got all steamed up about it and yelled at my father for an hour. My father just said sitting and reading was as good a way of staying out of trouble as he knew, so after that Flanagan never bothered me again.

Once he saw me just sitting and watching him set

up beers, and he got annoyed and said, "What are you looking at?"

I said, "I'm just looking at the beers when you set them up. I like the way they look."

Maybe he thought I was kidding him or something, because he looked at the beers and then he looked at me as if I was crazy. "What's there to like about the way they look!"

I said, "The way the head comes up from the bottom of the glass right after you fill it. It comes up so slow and easy and it rocks up and down until it comes all the way to the top."

So all he said was, "You got stones in the head," and he didn't bother about it any more. But I think he got to like it too, because now and then I would see him watching the glasses right after he filled them, and shaking his head.

Flanagan thought my father was just about the greatest man in the world. He would say to the regulars when my father wasn't around, "Andy LaMain is good-looking and smart and he has more brains than the Pope," and if one of them asked why, Flanagan would say, "Because he keeps his mouth shut."

Sometimes the guy would want to argue about this, but Flanagan would just say, "Aw, you got stones in the head," and wait on somebody else.

It was all right with me because I thought the same way. My father was small, a head smaller than me, but he was nice-looking and he had a good build. He had smooth black hair just getting a little gray in front, and a little mustache he used to trim by himself every morning in front of the mirror. And Flanagan was right about my father keeping quiet. He was the quietest man I ever knew.

He could stand behind the bar all day, and never say more than hello to the regulars. If they got into a battle about politics or something, he would just go to the other end of the bar and read the paper. Mostly, if there wasn't trade, or just enough so Flanagan could handle it all right by himself, my father would stand looking out of the window.

He was like that with Frances too. She would walk along holding his arm and talking away a mile a minute, and then when she stopped he would say maybe one, two words, and that was all. I think he gave her the feeling sometimes that he wasn't listening, because once she got me alone up in the rooms.

"Listen, George," she said, "I want to ask you something and I want it to be just between you and me."

"Sure," I said.

She was biting her thumbnail and looking at me like she was trying to figure out how to say it. "Look," she finally said, "does your father ever talk about me? I mean, does he ever say *anything* about me when I'm not around?"

I said, "No," and then she got scared and said, "Now remember, George, this was strictly between us."

She didn't have to say that, because I wouldn't have told him anyhow. I mean, you didn't just go and tell my father anything until he asked you, and even then he didn't seem interested. About once a month he would say to me, "Is everything all right at school?" and I would say yes, it was, and in between those times he would just give me my allowance or tell me to get a haircut. I hardly ever talked to my father. I think I was a little afraid of him.

But when he was laying on the floor with Flanagan slopping whisky over him, everything turned upside down in me. I wasn't afraid of him any more. I didn't even have any use for him. A guy had walked in out of nowhere and handed him a licking and he just laid down and took it. With everybody looking at him he stripped down and took a beating like a kid. When I got up from the table and saw all the people pushing around and him laying there, all I thought of was if he couldn't handle Al Judge, I could.

I wasn't a kid any more. I was big. Bigger than anybody standing around there with their stupid mouths hanging open, because I knew something they didn't. I knew that I was going to kill Al Judge. Kill him right away so there wouldn't be any mistake about why it happened, but do it so smart and slick that nobody in the world could put the finger on me.

And the biggest thing. Al Judge had to know before he died why it was happening. He had to get down on his knees in front of me just the way the Jews used to get down in front of the Nazis when they were going to get theirs. And he had to slobber all over me before the finish. Maybe I would get him all undressed first so that's the way the cops would find him.

Just that idea made me feel bigger than the whole world. My glasses were bent anyhow. I stuck them in my pocket and I went over to the people standing there and started to shove them. "Get out of here," I said; "Get out of here."

One of them started to shove me back, but another one grabbed him. "It's only right," he said. "Let them alone."

So one by one, pushing against each other with their heads still turned back to see, they started to jam out of the door through the people who were crowded around there. The last guy still had some of his beer left and he drank it down before he went out. Then they were all gone and I pushed against the door to get it shut, and then I locked it. After that I pulled down the shade over the door and the big shade over the window, and we were all alone.

CHAPTER THREE

FIFTEEN OR sixteen is a bad age for a kid.

I don't only mean because of the way the juice percolates in him and makes him all jumpy about girls and stuff, even if that is one of the worst things about it. I mean when you're fifteen, sixteen, you're right in the middle of nowhere.

Take a little kid. He can be the worst little punk on the block, but everybody says, "Isn't he cute! Where does he get all the energy! Isn't he full of the devil!" and they make all kinds of fuss over him.

Or take a guy gets to be near eighteen. He's big stuff. He smokes right in front of everybody. Maybe he lays a girl. And when his old man brings him into the bar, everybody says, "He's a better man than his pa," and they buy him a beer.

But a kid fifteen, sixteen, is a pain all around and mostly to himself.

He always opens his mouth at the wrong time, and he always says the wrong thing, and he's always doing the wrong thing. And it's not only that everybody else picks on him, but it's like he was always walking around with a mirror in front of him, and a phonograph playing back everything he says. He knows he's acting dumb, but he just can't seem to straighten himself out.

I think part of it is girls. First they're only like washboards running around on sticks and then all of a sudden they're all curves and lipstick, and every time you see a nice one you get all red in the face and think how it would be to grab her.

But that is only part of it. The other part is the way a smart kid like me could never open up and let people know how smart he was. I think sometimes it was worse than the girls.

You know how it is when two people start talking to each other and each one is talking about something different but they don't know it, and you do? If you're big you can step in and straighten everything out and maybe get right into the middle of the talk. But if you're a kid you just have to listen and swallow it. It sticks like a lump in you, but you swallow it just the same.

I read a lot of books, and plenty of times I could have

straightened guys out, but the only time I tried it they said, "Shut up, kid," and shoved me away. I never tried it again.

But when I was pushing everybody out of the bar and pulling down the shades, I was making up for all the lumps I swallowed. I was bigger than they were. I told them what to do, and they did it. That was the best time in my whole life up to then, and it all happened because I knew I was going to kill Al Judge. When you're going to kill somebody, you're not a kid any more, and when you know in your heart you're not a kid, somehow or other, everybody else seems to know it too.

After I pulled down the shades I went back to the end of the bar where Flanagan was helping my father get up. When he got up, he sort of leaned on the bar and shook his head hard. Then Flanagan filled half a short beer glass with the rest of the whisky from the bottle, and my father slugged it all down in one drink. I had a good look at his back then, and when I saw it my stomach knotted up in me, and my heart started to bang so loud I was afraid they would hear it too. It shortened up my breath for a minute so I could hardly take in air.

It was all stripes, so big they stood out like purple ropes. There was a mess of blood too, and some of it had run down on his belt and pants. There was whisky splashed all over his pants too, and it smelled bad. Whisky doesn't smell when you pour it in a glass, but just knock over a bottle and you can smell it from one end of a room to the other.

My father was a classy dresser. I mean, even when he was working the bar he would wear a good pair of pants, and they had to be pressed just so. And the first thing I thought was that the blood and whisky had sure ruined those pants, and he would be plenty mad about it. Then I remembered he wasn't mad about the whole thing, only yellow, taking it and not doing anything about it, and I got so mad I forgot and talked to him like he was some dumb little kid.

"Why did you let him do it?" I yelled. "What did you let him do it for?"

I thought Flanagan was going to hit me across the face. "Shut up!" he yelled. "Have you got stones in the head?"

I grabbed the glasses out of my pocket and tried to put them on. It feels funny talking to somebody without your glasses on when you're used to them. Only they were all twisted and my hands were shaking so much I couldn't get them fixed right.

My father didn't say anything at all. He took his underwear top and started to lift his arms to put it on, but it must have hurt too much. He put it down and picked up his shirt. Flanagan held it so he could slide his arms in. He stood there looking at the ceiling with his eyes shut while Flanagan buttoned the shirt and shoved it into his pants.

I said, "Aren't you going to get even with him? Even if he is a big shot, are you going to let him get away with it?"

Flanagan untied the apron and pulled it off, and my father turned around and looked at me. "Forget it."

I said, "What do you think everybody on the block is talking about now? Why don't you go and tell them to forget it too?"

Flanagan grabbed my shoulder. "What do you mean, talking to your father like that!" but my father said, "Let him go, Flanagan."

I pulled away anyhow. "Maybe you think I'm still a kid! Well, I'm not! If Flanagan wasn't holding me down before I would have jumped that guy myself! And I will anyhow, only when I do it there won't be anybody around to bother me!"

And right there it was like the mirror and the phonograph were in front of me, only for once it felt good. It made me feel just like my muscles were made out of iron and my mind was like a needle, sharp and shiny, thinking the right things to say and to do so nothing could go wrong. That's the way grown-ups feel, and why they can walk around the way they do without worrying every second about what they say or do. It's a wonderful feeling.

Even the way my father looked at me couldn't take the edge off that feeling, because he didn't know I was going to kill Al Judge, so maybe to him it was still a kid talking. And if my father never did know I was the one who killed Al Judge, I would know it all right, and that was enough.

So all my father said to me was, "Forget it," and then he said to Flanagan, "Close up the place. I'm going upstairs."

We waited, just standing there, while Flanagan checked the lock on the door, then took the dirty glasses off the bar and dumped them into a tub of water. Then he took out the cashbox from under the bar and dumped all the money from the cash register in it without even counting it. After that he pulled the strings oh the two big lights and turned on the night light so that everything turned into shadows and dirt and made knowing I was going to kill Al Judge something like in a movie, only real.

There was a back door to the bar, and it opened on a little hallway with stairs going up to our apartment. We all went into the hallway with my father carrying his underwear shirt, and Flanagan carrying the cashbox.

Before we went upstairs, Flanagan opened the back door which opened on a little yard, only it was cement instead of dirt, and he called, "Kitty, kitty, kitty."

Nothing happened, so he called, "Pss, pss, pss," until a big old she-cat came running in. She didn't have any real name, only Kitty, and she wasn't even Flanagan's cat. She was just a mangy little thing once, and he picked her up and took care of her until she ran away. But she still hung around a lot, and every night he would try to get her into the bar so she would catch rats there.

He said the nights she ran in meant there was going to be rain, so she was better than the weather reports on the radio, but it mostly didn't work out like that. When I showed him a couple of times it didn't work out right, he said that meant it was ready to rain but it cleared up overnight. I think he started the whole thing for a joke and then he really got to believe it.

The cat came running in and Flanagan closed the back door behind her, but before he closed it I had a good look outside. It was windy out, and starting to get cold, and the old tree in Ehrlich's yard next door was shaking so hard it looked like it was getting ready to pull out of the ground and take off. Mr. Ehrlich kept the candy store next door, and the tree was his peach tree, and he used to take care of it all year round. He used to fuss around with his glasses sliding down his nose, cutting off dead parts and pulling out leaves here and there, and even watering the ground when it didn't rain for a long time. You'd think it was his own kid.

For all his work, he never got any peaches off it. Near the end of the summer some hard little peaches would show up, and as soon as they got ripe the kids from the block would swipe them. But Mr. Ehrlich never quit trying.

The tree was seesawing back and forth, and a couple of newspaper pages came flying along and plastered up against the fence and started flapping there, and that was all I could see because it was so dark out.

Than Flanagan closed the door, and my father started going up the stairs very slowly with me behind him and Flanagan in back of me. From the way my father walked I knew it was hard for him climbing those stairs and I could feel tears in my eyes because of it. But underneath, I felt hot and strong because Flanagan was only carrying the cashbox up, and not the revolver that lay right in back of it in the big drawer.

It was important, because that was the revolver I was going to use tonight.

CHAPTER FOUR

When you got to the top of the stairs, you were standing right outside the parlor door in the front part of the house. If you walked back along the hall there instead of going into the parlor, next was the bedroom, then the bathroom, and then the kitchen where you could look into the back yard. The parlor was my room, and the bedroom was my father's room.

There was a great big double door between the parlor and the bedroom. Big enough so if you opened it all the way it would be almost like one big room, but I never saw it opened. Sometimes I woke up very late at night because there was talking and noise in the bedroom, but those big double doors were so tight together you couldn't see through the crack what was going on.

Mostly in the morning my father was sleeping when

I had to go to school, so I made my breakfast and pulled out as quiet as I could. But Saturday and Sunday I would get up late, and we would have breakfast together, and then he would take his paper and read it by the front window in the parlor. He sat in the big armchair and he had his feet on a little chair, and for about an hour all you could see was cigarette smoke coming up out of the newspaper.

Sometimes I had something important to talk to him about, but I learned to wait until he was all done with the paper. Then, while he was getting on a clean apron to go down and open the bar, I would say what I had to.

The parlor was the best room in the house. All the other rooms only had linoleum on the floor, but the parlor had a real carpet. It didn't have a real bed, but the day bed was plenty good enough for me and it was easier to keep fixed up. When I was in the Boy Scouts I used to fix up the day bed every morning with the sheet straight and the blankets good and tight, but after I quit the Boy Scouts it didn't seem to matter so I didn't bother any more. When Frances came up she would yell about it and straighten up the day bed and my father's bed and dust around. I didn't mind her yelling, because if she dusted around she saved me the trouble.

In the parlor there was the armchair and the day bed, a big bureau, some plain chairs, and a little rickety table that was no good at all, except the radio was on it and my grandfather's picture.

Once when I was a dumb little kid I picked up the frame with my grandfather's picture to look at it better, and right behind it in the frame. I saw there was some other picture. I dug around with my fingers until I could pull it out, and then I saw it was a picture of my mother. I remembered a little about my mother, and somehow I knew right off this was her picture.

I got a creepy feeling when I saw it, because around the house we never talked about my mother, and it was like seeing spooks or something. So without even thinking, I took it into the bedroom to show to my father. He was just getting up, and he was sitting on the edge of the bed rubbing his hair when I went in. I held out the picture and said, "Look, I found Ma's picture."

For a second he looked like he was standing in heavy traffic with a truck coming at him and not able to get out of the way. Then he took the picture out of my hand and started to tear little pieces off it. He tore and tore until there was no more picture at all, just little pieces laying all around him on the floor. Then he said through his teeth, "Get out of here!" and I was so scared I ran out almost bawling.

He didn't come out after me either. He shut the door

and stayed there so long that Flanagan had to open the bar and get everything fixed up.

Afterwards I was sorry about the picture because my mother was so pretty. She had a ribbon around her hair and big eyes a little slanty. In the picture she was turned away a little so it looked like she was smiling back at you. And the way she was smiling was different too. It wasn't like the silly kind of a smile most people have when they're getting their picture taken. It was more like she was laughing at something she knew but you didn't know.

Afterwards I started snooping around but I never found another picture of her anywhere.

CHAPTER FIVE

THE TWO big orange tickets, almost as big as post cards, were laying right in the middle of the dresser.

Funny how something big can chase everything else out of your mind. First it was the fights, and from the time my father told me I was going I couldn't get it out of my head.

When I was washing in front of the bathroom mirror, I would stop right in the middle to make like I was Rocks Abruzzo slamming one into Joe Shotfield's face. Then I was Joe Shotfield trying to come out of it and I would cover up but Rocks would be all over me. I would start to go down, but then I was back being Rocks again and I was standing there while Joe was counted out.

I read about it in all the papers I could get hold of, and I even told some of the kids around the school and it went over big with them. It was the most important thing that happened to me.

But from the time Al Judge walked into the bar, I never thought about it. It just wasn't in my mind. Too much was happening, and even walking up the stairs so slow with my father and Flanagan I didn't think about it, because near the top my father started to let go, and if I didn't grab him and Flanagan get an arm around him, he might have gone all the way down again on his head.

When we got him into the bedroom he dropped flat on his belly on the bed like a dead one. I got scared, but after Flanagan switched on the light and put the cashbox down, he gave him a once-over and said he was okay, only hurt bad. I knew that all right; Flanagan didn't have to tell it me.

Then I saw the tickets on the dresser, and so many things came into my mind at once I couldn't straighten them out. It wasn't that I cared about not going to be fights, because after what happened it didn't seem important any more. But then it hit me right between the eyes that Al Judge would be at the fights. He had to write about it, didn't he? And all I could see was him sitting at the ringside with the back of his head lined right up in the sights of the revolver. Then *pow!* and he drops right down over the typewriter. If I waited for when there was real action in the fight and plenty of noise and excitement, nobody would ever know it was me who did it.

There was a movie I saw where a guy was gunning for one of the prizefighters just that way. I couldn't think right then if he got away with it or not because the next thought that tangled me up was if I killed Al Judge like that, he wouldn't know why it happened, and the big thing was he had to know why it happened before he went.

Besides, what was the use of knocking myself out over that, because if my father was hurt and couldn't go to the fights, I knew I wasn't going either. But I *had* to go. If I didn't kill Al Judge right there, I could still keep an eye on him. Then after the fights I could shadow him until I got him in the right spot. Otherwise I might never find out where he was, and before I could it would be too late.

Those tickets cost eight dollars apiece too, and that would be an awful waste.

I picked up the tickets and stood there looking at them with my head buzzing round and round, and it was Flanagan who fixed everything up without even meaning to. He went into the bathroom, and I heard the water squirting into the bathtub. Then he came back and gave my father a boost so he was sitting up on the edge of the bed. I think maybe that shot of whisky had taken hold too, because my father's eyes were as big and shiny as marbles and he hardly seemed to know what was going on.

Flanagan started to peel his shirt off and said, "A nice warm tub, Andy, and you'll feel like the jack of trump. Then we'll get some stuff on that back and roll you to bed."

I don't think my father knew what Flanagan said. He sat there looking at the wall like he was trying to remember something. Then he said, "I'm a little tired, that's all. A little tired," and Flanagan helped him get on his feet and said, "Sure, sure, Andy, the tub is all ready now."

Then they got started into the bathroom very slow, and I heard the door close and a lot of splashing, so I figured he was in the bathtub.

In all my life I never did anything my father told me not to. That little sip of beer didn't count because Flanagan said it was tasting and not drinking. But in all the big things I did what my father wanted. Like the kids on the block had a Halloween party or something and he said don't go, I didn't go. I might be a little sore about it, but I didn't let him know that.

When the kids used to go down Ehrlich's cellar and monkey around with girls, I mean not even the works, just feeling around and looking, I wanted to go more than anything else in the world. Only some drunk in the bar started talking about it, and my father told me not to do it. So I didn't do that either. And I didn't smoke and I only cursed when I forgot, because on my block it didn't even sound like cursing. I mean, some kid would want to say it's a very hot day, and he would say it's a f——ing hot day and you wouldn't even notice. Everybody did it, and they laughed at me because I tried not to. I think I was a pretty good kid.

That's why I'm glad my father didn't think about the fights and maybe say something to me about not going. Because I was going to do something he wouldn't like anyhow, and if he told me straight out not to do it, it would make it that much worse. I would do it even if he told me not to, but it would have been the first time, and I would feel bad about it. This way was much better.

I stood still for a long time in front of the dresser, but all I heard was a little mumbling and splashing. I was wearing a sweater and I slipped it off. My father and I kept all our clothes in the bedroom closet together, his on the right-hand side, and mine on the left. I swung open the closet door so it wouldn't squeak and got out a necktie and put it on. Then I got my suit coat out and my overcoat. When I had them on, I took my good hat and bent the brim down in front. Even so, when I peeked in the mirror, it looked like a kid's hat. I put it back and took out my father's hat. It was black with a real snap brim, and I looked good in it. Like a man. I knew because I already tried it on.

When I was all dressed except for some buttons, I looked out in the hall, but everything was okay. I sneaked out as far as the stairs and then I remembered the tickets. It would have been a nice pickle if I went all the way up to Madison Square Garden and didn't even have a ticket to get in. I went back into the room, grabbed the tickets, and looked at the clock. It was only quarter to nine, so I had plenty of time to get to the fights before they broke up. It would only take ten, fifteen minutes in the Ninth Avenue bus.

When I got out to the stairs again, I was soaked with sweat through and through. The house was pretty warm, and the coat was heavy, and besides that, I was sick with the feeling I had to go out and get it over with. I felt my face and it felt flaming hot but that was maybe because my hand was all ice-cold and wet. I wondered if I was getting sick with anything serious.

I went down the stairs on the side by the wall where it wasn't so squeaky. Even so, the house was so quiet that every step I took sounded like a fire alarm to me. When I got to the bottom it was pitch-black there, so I had to feel around for the door-knob. Once I got the door open it was better, because the night light was on in the bar.

It was a funny feeling walking through the bar. On the table where I was eating supper was the plate with the steak bone on it and a couple of French fried potatoes. I picked one up but it felt somehow like a dead man's finger might and I dropped it quick. The book was there too. I picked it up and put it down under the bar where I kept it.

Then I went to the cash register and opened the big drawer under it. The gun was there all right; I could hear it scrape a little when I pulled the drawer out. I reached it and took it out, and it felt colder and heavier than I could ever remember. It didn't feel like it could kill anybody. It just felt like a big heavy tool. Like a monkey wrench or something.

I stuck it in my right-hand overcoat pocket, but the pocket was too small and the butt stuck out. So I pulled it out, and then I remembered I didn't even look to see if it was loaded. I broke it open the way Flanagan did when he cleaned it, and there were bullets in every chamber. I closed it up, and this time I stuck it into my right-hand pants pocket, because it was pretty big.

I must have shoved too hard or something, because the next thing I knew there was a rip and the barrel went right through my pants. It felt like a piece of ice rubbing along my leg, and I pulled at it but the front sight must have caught in the pocket because I could hardly get it out, and when I did there wasn't much pocket left. My glasses were all smashed too on the floor. I forgot about them in my pocket and now they were done for, but good. I just let them lay there.

I was going to put the gun in my other pants pocket then, but the thought of having it on the left-hand side was so uncomfortable in my mind that I just stuck it right back in the torn pocket. It stayed in there all right, only the barrel was against my leg cold as death.

Then I buttoned up and went around to the door. I didn't have my key with me, so I fixed the lock to stay open. It didn't matter what with the money upstairs. Then I remembered something. I had the tickets and the gun, but I didn't have any money along. And the money box was upstairs.

For a second I figured on going back to the bedroom and taking some money out of the box, but then maybe my luck would run out and Flanagan or my father would see me. Anyhow I could get a dime from Mr. Ehrlich in the candy store, because he would always lend you a dime if you needed it.

I took a quick look from the corner of the window shade to see if anybody was hanging around the front of the bar, but nobody was there. When I opened the door, the wind was so bad it nearly pulled it out of my hand and banged it against the wall. I just grabbed it in time. Then I pulled it shut and stepped out into the street.

There was dust and stuff blowing along so hard it stung my eyes. All up and down the block you could hear the tin signs banging back and forth, and I saw that Mr. Ehrlich had taken all the papers off the news stand. He only did that in bad weather or on Halloween night when the kids were out for a good time, so the papers wouldn't get spoiled. He would stack them up on the candy counter in the store then, and all the guys who wanted a free look would crowd in and you could hardly breathe.

When I thought of the guys in there, and what they would be saying about my father, I almost felt like not going in. But I needed that dime bad, so I had to. I didn't waste any time. I ran over to the door of the candy store and pushed it open. There were plenty of guys in there all right, getting their free look, and the first one to get a good look at me was Kennealy, the new cop on the beat.

CHAPTER SIX

For a slow count of five I stood there frozen, with my back pasted up against the door. Maybe it's a lucky thing I froze up like that, because if I didn't I might have gone right out through the door again and then Kennealy would sure have started to smell something fishy.

Kennealy was a new cop, and old Mr. Reardon who was retired on a pension and hung around the bar every night for a couple of hours used to say new cops were always funny the way they went looking for trouble. They figured maybe they could become heroes and get on plain-clothes, so they went around stirring up what they couldn't see. Besides, I always used to tighten up around cops. I could walk down the street not doing a thing and when a cop came by and gave me the eye

I would feel just like a crook and I could feel the way I was walking and looking, I looked just like a crook too.

And there I was standing without my glasses and with my father's good hat shoved on my head, and that big gun scraping along my leg, and knowing in my head I was going to kill Al Judge, watching Kennealy look at me. He was standing in front of the soda fountain with a glass of seltzer and chocolate in one hand and a marshmallow cracker that was half gone in the other hand. When he first saw me he was sloshing the soda around in the glass, I guess to mix it up, then after he got a good look he drank it all down and waved the glass at me to come over.

I walked over very slow and all I knew was if he tried anything funny like frisking me or something, I would pull away and try to get the gun out and let him have it. I didn't even get started on what I was going to do, and no cop was going to spoil it right off. There wasn't any reason why he would even think of frisking me, but that didn't stop me from thinking the way I did.

When I got near him, he said, "Hey, LaMain, what's this I hear about your old man getting beat up tonight?"

When he said that, everybody else turned around to take a look at me. There was Mr. Ehrlich with his glasses slipping down his nose looking worried, and maybe three, four other guys from the block, and they all looked at me. One of the guys said, "Yeah, an eyewitness came up to the whore house and told Kennealy all about it, so now he's coming around to investigate," and everybody laughed except Mr. Ehrlich. He didn't like that kind of talk around the store, because sometimes Mrs. Ehrlich was there, and maybe Gertrude, the baby.

I said, "He got beat up, but he said to forget it."

The same guy made a face like he smelled something bad and said, "He must of had it coming to him, all right," but another one said, "Andy is okay. Maybe he figures to square it his own way," and that got a rise out of Kennealy.

He said very hot, "As long as this is my beat we don't want any of that stuff around here. Is that what he's got on his mind, LaMain?"

"No. He said to forget it."

One of the guys made a loud raspberry. "Go on. Al Judge is too big for him. If he ever started anything, the whole circulation gang of the *Press* would be down here to take his joint apart."

Kennealy waved his hand at the guy to shut him up, and then he waved his empty seltzer-and-chocolate glass at me. "Look, kid. You tell your old man I know what happened and I know who was in it, and if anything more comes out of it, I'll know just where to start looking. You tell him that, kid."

One of the guys said, "What's the matter, Kennealy, you figure on Al Judge to get you a promotion?" and they all started laughing again.

Only Mr. Ehrlich didn't. He leaned over the counter and said very worried, "How is he now, Georgie? Is he hurt bad?"

I said, "He's all right, only he's laying down and I don't want to bother him. So please, Mr. Ehrlich, could you lend me a dime?"

The same guy made a raspberry again and said, "He's an expert at laying down, ain't he?" and I thought someday I'll get that guy and get him good. I wouldn't even kill him, just beat him up with a lead pipe or something until there wasn't one little piece left whole, and then I'd just kick him in the face laying there in front of me. Only that wasn't the important thing then. Getting my dime and getting out of there was the important thing.

But before I could get the dime, I heard Mrs. Ehrlich yelling down the back steps, "Meyer. Meyer. If that's Georgie, send him up please. Tell him it's important."

More than anything in the world, I didn't want to go upstairs then, because I knew what Mrs. Ehrlich wanted. Every now and then, she went out to do shopping or maybe to a movie, and she was afraid little Gertrude might wake up and start crying. So she would give me a dime, maybe a quarter, just to sit upstairs and read until she came back. It was all right with me because that meant I could take new comic books and stuff up from the magazine rack as long as I put them back when I went out. But tonight I only wanted to get started, and going upstairs would spoil it.

I started to tell Mr. Ehrlich I had to go somewhere but he put out his hands and smiled. "Look, I'll give you the dime. But do me a favor. It's only for a couple of minutes so she can go shopping."

It was no good to start arguing. With everybody around I was only afraid they would wonder what was so important and maybe start to ask questions. One of them even said, "What is it, Georgie? Got a big date tonight?" but instead of saying anything, I pushed around them and went upstairs.

Mrs. Ehrlich was standing at the top of the stairs. She was short and kind of dumpy with two big bloopers, but she had a nice face and she was always smiling.

"Oh good, good," she said right away, "Georgie, I got to go shopping maybe ten, fifteen minutes. I promise I'll be back quick. Meanwhile keep an eye on the baby, huh?"

Sometimes she would say that and it would be an hour before she came back. So I said, "Look, Mrs. Ehrlich, my father is hurt and I have to get back right away. So please hurry up if you don't mind."

She put her hands to her head. "Oh, I heard about it. Such a nice man, and such a terrible thing to happen. Is he hurt bad, Georgie? Did you have a doctor?"

I said, "He's hurt pretty bad, Mrs. Ehrlich, and I have to be back right away. So please hurry up."

I went into the parlor and she went to get her coat, and all the time she was putting it on she kept saying, "Terrible. Terrible. Such a neighborhood," until I wanted to tell her to shut up. Then she ran down the stairs and I sat down in my overcoat to wait.

I know one thing always happens to me when I get all hot and bothered like before I take a big test in school. I have to take a leak bad. Even if I went only a little while before, I still feel I have to go again, and sometimes I'll go three or four times in a row without anything happening, only I have the feeling.

That's how I felt while I was sitting there and waiting, so I got up and went down the hall to the bathroom and it wasn't any false alarm either. Only when I got done I still had the feeling and my knees were trembling like there was a wind blowing through them. And the funniest thing was when I put my hand in my pants pocket to straighten out the gun because it was poking me, all the feeling went away.

I pulled out the gun and went over to the mirror and pointed it right at my face in the mirror. I couldn't see too good but the black hat looked good and I made a face like a tough guy pointing the gun at it. Only the mirror was so high that if I wanted to see the gun I had to hold it way up in the air and that made it look phony.

I turned out the bathroom light and held the gun under my coat. Then I tiptoed out into the hall and into the bedroom where the door was open. There was a big dresser in the bedroom with a mirror that you could see everything in from your belt up. The baby's crib was in there too, so I was very quiet and instead of turning on the overhead light I switched on the lamp by the bed. The bedroom smelled funny like baby's pee and some sweet powder but that didn't matter. I pointed the gun at myself in the mirror and it was so good I could see Al Judge standing in front of me there, with the sweat running down his face. The only trouble was, the way it looked in the mirror he had a gun too and that spoiled it.

Then all of a sudden there was a loud noise and I tried to turn around and shove the gun under my coat at the same time. But it was only little baby Gertrude crying because maybe the light bothered her or something. I couldn't even move for a minute until I got everything straightened out in my head, and then I took the gun out from under my coat and went to the crib.

The baby was pushing her arms out over her head and

yelling loud, and every time she did it I had that feeling of somebody pulling his fingernail down a blackboard. I put my hand tight over her mouth so all you could hear was the noise pushing inside of her. All I could think of was somehow she would tell about me and the gun, and then I remembered she didn't even know how to talk yet and I pulled my hand away.

She started to yell all over again, and I took the gun and pointed it right at her head. I said, "Shut up, or I'll give it to you."

That was some feeling. I think I had her all mixed up with Al Judge in my mind and I was giving it to him.

I wanted to do it now so bad that it was like hot waves in my stomach. I kept the gun pointing at her, and I pulled back the hammer with my thumb till it clicked. Then I started pulling on the trigger, but careful, so the gun wouldn't go off. And then all of a sudden, baby Gertrude stopped crying and I felt everything loosen up in me so I didn't want to kid around any more.

But now I had the hammer back and I didn't know how to get it closed again. I couldn't think of what to do, and I was afraid to put the gun in my pocket that way because it might go off. All I could think of was putting the safety on, and that was better than nothing even though I would rather have the hammer back where it belonged. And just then I heard Mrs. Ehrlich coming up the stairs. I shoved the gun away in my pocket and tried to pull my coat straight, and I stood by the crib looking at baby Gertrude so that when Mrs. Ehrlich came in she would find me like that. She came in with two big bundles in her arms, and right away she looked scared.

"What's wrong, Georgie? What happened?" She dumped the two bags down on the bed and started to pat her hand all over the baby's face.

I said, "She was crying so I came in to see what it was. Then she stopped right away."

Mrs. Ehrlich said, "Oh, I got scared." Then she smiled all over and said, "You're a real little father, Georgie. The girl who gets you, she'll be the lucky one all right."

Then she patted the kid some more and pulled her straight. After that she turned out the light and got her packages to take in the kitchen. In the hall she said, "And tell your father, Georgie, he should feel better, and he's got a wonderful, wonderful boy."

All the way down the stairs I was worried about the guys standing around, but when I came in there was only one left, and he was reading the paper and didn't even look up. Mr. Ehrlich gave me a dime and I put it in my overcoat pocket. He said, "Give your father my best, Georgie, and tell him to take care of himself," and I said, "Okay, Mr. Ehrlich," and I went out into the street.

I pushed up my coat collar and I shoved my hands into my overcoat pocket and started walking as fast as I could away from the candy store and the bar. I figured it would be better to take a bus a block away in case Flanagan or my father was by the window upstairs.

Down the block was Mr. Triola's barbershop where I got haircuts, and there was a clock in back of the store. I tried to see what time it was, but it was too dark inside. I figured it must be getting pretty near time for the big fight, because it started at ten o'clock after the preliminaries.

The big fight always went on at ten o'clock so they could broadcast it over the radio. I always used to listen to them over the radio and wonder what it was really like to see them, and now I was going to find out. That was all right, but it was even better when I thought how Al Judge would be sitting by the ringside maybe writing something about the fight, and I would be sitting up in the first row of the mezzanine watching him, and any time I wanted to kill him I could. I was his boss only he didn't know it.

But I didn't want to kill him there. I wanted to get him in the right spot and then it would be easy. That was one thing I found out when I was kidding around with baby Gertrude. It was going to be easier to kill somebody with a gun than I ever figured.

CHAPTER SEVEN

As soon as I got off the bus at Fiftieth Street at the back end of Madison Square Garden, I tightened up. Al Judge was somewhere around here. Maybe he was inside watching the preliminaries wind up, but you couldn't be sure. He might be walking right behind me looking down my neck. He could be standing in a dark spot by the building watching me go by and I wouldn't know. He could be anywhere around me now, and that's what tightened me up.

I tried to figure out if he would know who I was from seeing me in the bar. He might have seen me good but he might have been too excited to get it stuck in his head. I didn't remember him looking my way, but I was out for a while too, and he might have noticed then. But when a guy is out with his face down on the table, it's not easy to see what he looks like. I started to figure suppose Sam Schwartz was with him when I caught up to him, Sam Schwartz would know me good. But what would Sam Schwartz be doing with him? It didn't make sense but it bothered me. All that kind of stuff.

I walked down Fiftieth to Eighth Avenue where the front entrance of the Garden was, and all the way I kept seeing Al Judge pop up in front of me. Once it was a big guy and he was wearing a white scarf, and then it was a guy who limped but he didn't have a cane, and the way I was starting and stopping and looking around, anybody who was watching me would have figured I was crazy sure.

When I got into the lobby of the Garden it was worse than ever. There was a lot of people liked Rocks Abruzzo because he was a killer, but I never figured on so many jamming into that street like, that goes right into the building and up to the ticket doors. Mostly men but with a couple of women and they were all pushing in and out so that you could hardly get through them. In that mob, Al Judge could have shoved right into me and I wouldn't know it. So all I could do was keep looking around as much as I could and hope it wouldn't happen like that.

I knew what Madison Square Garden looked like all right because I was there once before. That was the time Mr. Hildebrand from the C.Y.O. took a bunch of kids to the circus and my father gave me money to go along. First we went down in the basement where they had all the freaks sitting around and it was all right. I mean the way there were so many different freaks and you could walk around and look at them and they didn't even mind. It was a break I was so tall, too, because the other kids had to hop up and down to get a look until somebody let them get up front where they could see.

But then the kids started acting crazy and saying all kinds of things right out in front of the freaks and that spoiled it. A lot of people laughed and Mr. Hildebrand laughed too, and the freaks looked like they didn't care, but inside of me I remembered how it was when I pulled something dumb in school and the teacher would yell at me and I would sit and look just like the freaks were doing. I mean looking over everybody's head like they weren't there and maybe smiling a little bit like it was funny or something. But inside it hurt all the way down.

So that spoiled it for me, and when we went upstairs to where the real circus was with the acrobats and clowns and stuff I didn't like it so much. I made believe I did but I really didn't.

But I knew what Madison Square Garden looked like and how to get in. What scared me was somebody in the crowd would shove up against the gun and feel it was a gun and maybe start trouble. So I put my hand over it in my pocket as far as I could, and when anybody pushed into me they would only feel my hand.

The only thing I wished was that I could let them know what I had in my hand without getting into trouble and spoiling everything. If they knew I had a gun there they would give me plenty of room. They would fall over one another getting out of the way, and I would walk up the middle with everybody holding their breath. Just thinking about it like that made me feel real tough and I started to push through without caring what they said or the way they looked at me. The only thing was I kept my overcoat unbuttoned and my hand tight over the gun.

Near the end of this street in the building was a row of doors and a couple of guards taking tickets and letting a few people in, and that's where I headed. Everybody was pushing around but hardly anybody was trying to get in, and I caught on right away. They didn't have tickets and they couldn't even buy one any more. Then a skinny guy with a big beak grabbed my arm and said, "Buddy, got an extra ticket?" and I pulled away before I remembered I did have an extra ticket and it would go to waste. It didn't matter. I was getting close to Al Judge and that was the big thing. I wanted to get everything over and done with, and besides it made me jumpy to have anybody grab my arm that way.

I was near the guard and I got the tickets out. Before I could shove one away, another man grabbed my arm and pointed at it. He said, "If that's an extra, I'll pay plenty for it," and it hit me all of a sudden that the extra ticket was worth plenty of money and maybe it would come in handy. I mean, suppose Al Judge took it into his head to go around in a taxi somewhere. Then I would have to grab a taxi too, and I would need money for it. All I had was the nickel left from the bus fare.

The man who stopped me was wearing very good clothes, you could see that right off, and under his hat you could see red hair, and he had a little bristly red mustache too. He looked all right to me so I said, "How much?"

I don't know if it happens to other people but it happens to me sometime. I mean, now and then you meet a guy, you take a look at him, and you know he's all right. It sort of shows through.

That's the way I felt about this man. Maybe it was because he looked so clean. He looked like he scrubbed an hour and then put on a brand new suit. Everything on him was clean and flat and pressed right, the way my father liked it. Only he didn't wear a hat like my father. He wore a pearl-gray fedora without any dent in it except the one down the middle, and the brim turned up all around. On somebody else it might look corny, but on him it looked all right. I thought he would say right off how much he would give me for the ticket but he didn't. He said, "Let's see the ticket and I'll make you an offer."

I showed him the ticket and he whistled. "Hey, that's all right. Is it a deal for ten bucks?"

I said, "Okay," and he opened his wallet and took out a ten-dollar bill like you would expect him to carry around. It was so new it was hardly wrinkled. I stalled a second to look at it before I folded it up, and that's when it happened. Somebody slammed a hand hard on my shoulder, and said in my ear, "Okay, big boy. You're it."

All I knew was Al Judge had grabbed me when I wasn't ready. I almost yelled, it shocked me so much, but at the same time I twisted around as hard as I could and grabbed for the gun. Before I got my hand on it, I saw it wasn't Al Judge at all. It was a big fat red-faced guy, and he was plenty sore because I knocked his hat off when I twisted around. He grabbed at the hat with one hand, and got it on, and with the other hand he started to wrestle me away to the wall. I didn't even argue about it, I was so glad it wasn't Al Judge even if he was almost pulling my arm off. Everybody was getting in his way too and trying to look at us and he didn't like that either. He shoved right along until he got me in a corner where nobody was standing and then he flashed a badge at me so I knew he was a cop.

I didn't know what to do then. I couldn't run what with all the people blocking the way out, and I could hardly get at the gun because he had me crowded in so, and he might get suspicious if I made a quick grab for it again. I figured he must have seen the gun or felt it or something and that was why he pinched me, and then my mind started to go around like crazy trying to think of a good lie to tell him.

But he didn't frisk me. He didn't say anything about the gun. All he said was, "How much did you get for that ticket, Joe?"

I tried to tell him but it stuck in my throat so I held out the ten-dollar bill and he grabbed it and looked at it. He said, "That's all I want to know," and he shoved me hard up against the wall and almost leaned on top of me. "Don't you know you can't go around peddling tickets like that, bud? You ain't as dumb as all that, are you?"

There was a radiator up against the back of my legs, and it must have been red hot because I started to get all warm there and my whole body started to sweat. And he had his face right in mine and I could smell beer on him and it smelled awful. Only I was afraid to move my face away or my legs because it might make him sore, and if he moved one little inch he would be pushing right up against the gun. I tried to stand as still as I could, even with the radiator scorching through my pants, and I said, "I didn't know it was wrong to sell a ticket. Honest, mister, I wouldn't do it if I knew it was wrong. My father got two tickets, only he's sick so he couldn't come along with me. Honest, mister, I didn't know it was wrong."

I talked as fast as I could, and he stood there blowing that beer in my face and not even blinking his eyes. "Got any identification, Joe?"

I said, "No," and that was no lie. Everything was in the top dresser drawer. That was my drawer, and I knew my library card and my G.O. card from school were there, but all I had with me was the ticket and the gun. I was thinking fast. If I could shove him away with one hand, I could have a chance to get at the gun and make a break for it, and that was the only way I could see it. I would lay for Al Judge until the fights were over and then see if I could find him.

I started to let my right hand underneath my overcoat very slow, and the cop didn't notice. He said, "Where's your draft card? Don't you have sense enough to carry that around?"

I got my hand down into my pocket so my fingers touched the gun. My legs were burning so I didn't think I could stay like that much longer. I said, "I don't have any draft card. I'm not old enough."

I got a good grip on the gun and started to draw it out of the pocket with my thumb on the safety. I started to slip the safety off but I stopped. It was better to wait until I had the gun out of my pocket. The backs of my legs were so hot they were one pain up and down, but I braced them against the radiator, so that when I shoved I wouldn't be pushed off balance.

One second before I was ready to shove, he stepped back away from me and held out the ten-dollar bill. He said, "Bud, as long as I got this evidence here you're in plenty of trouble. But you know, if there wasn't no evidence there isn't a damn thing I could do. Got any ideas?"

Then I saw the way he was looking at me and I caught on. I said, "That isn't my money. I don't know anything about it."

He pushed his face close to mine again. "You sure?"

"I don't know anything about it."

"You picked it up when you seen it fall out of my pocket, didn't you?"

I said, "Yes, that's what happened."

He looked at the money, and then he folded it up

very small and shoved it into his pants pocket. "Bud, let me give you some advice. The next time you see somebody drop money, don't think about it so long before you give it back. Now go on, get the hell out of here."

My legs were so bad when I pulled away from the radiator that when the air hit my pants it felt like ice water. I didn't stop though, and I kept my hand on the gun while I walked over to the guard at the door. It felt like the cop was looking at the back of my neck every step I took. After I gave my ticket in and the guard tore it in half and gave me half back, I got up my nerve and looked around, but the cop was gone.

Then when I got into the lobby I bent and rubbed my hand up and down my legs because they felt like fire. And while I was doing that, it struck me for the first time maybe the guy wasn't a real cop after all. Maybe he was just a smart chiseler that got away with my ten dollars, and that made me hot all over.

If I only knew for sure he was a real cop I wouldn't care. I mean, all right, you pay off a cop, everybody does, and that's why guys want to be cops. But if a chiseler gets your money you're just dumb, and it shakes you all up inside.

CHAPTER EIGHT

I WAS getting close all right. I was on top of him now. He was sitting down there by the ring somewhere and before everybody started leaving and getting in my way I would be right after him and watch the way he went. I would tag him through the street or the subway or wherever he went. Maybe he would smell trouble and start to sweat. But if there was anybody around, it was still no good. He had to be alone, and even when I got him alone, I had to be careful because of that cane. I knew what he could do with that cane and I couldn't take any chances.

I leaned over the rail in front of my seat and tried to figure. His arm gave him about four feet, and the cane was good for another four. Then if he took a step, that was maybe two, three more. I added it up in my head and it came to ten, eleven feet, so the nearest I could come was twelve feet because I didn't want to take any chances.

Suppose he started to put up a fight before I got a chance to tell him what it was all about? I would have to plug him in the belly then, so he could hang on a little while and I could tell him. Then I would put in the finisher.

The big clock on the wall said ten o'clock, because the last preliminary was over and the main bout was ready to go on. That meant they were putting it on the radio too, and maybe Flanagan was sitting there and listening. He was a bug on fights, and if he got my father to bed all right he would sit in the parlor and listen. But what if my father got worried and they started looking for me? They would know easy where I was because the tickets were gone. The best thing would be if the fight was over right away and I could get going.

Only what worried me was finding Al Judge down there. There was no fighting in the ring, only a lot of guys walking around and talking, and plenty of light. Once the fight started, it would be even harder to find him, and it was plenty tough enough now without my glasses.

I started looking at one corner of the ring and I

looked all around the four sides trying to count heads, but I could hardly make anything out. Then I saw the man next to me was looking through a little pair of field glasses, not big ones like Mr. Reardon had for the races but little ones, and I figured I would ask for a lend of them. When I started to ask, I saw it was the redheaded man I sold my ticket to.

That shows how dumb you can be sometimes when you're all hot and bothered. I mean, he was using my other ticket so of course he would be sitting next to me, and I hadn't even thought about it until I saw him there.

He had his hat on his lap and he was looking through the glasses very busy, and his hair was about the way I figured it, short with a little wave in it and very red. When I started asking for the glasses he took them down, then he took a good look at me and grabbed my hand and shook it. His hand was very soft and smooth but he had a good grip. He said, "Well, I'm glad to see you. I saw that guy grab you right after I got inside the door, and I was wondering if I got you into any kind of mess. What was it all about?"

I said, "He was sore because I sold my ticket. He said I wasn't supposed to." I was almost starting to spill what I figured out about the guy maybe being a chiseler and not even a cop, but I stopped myself. It wasn't anybody's business anyhow, so I only said, "Could I take a look through your glasses?"

He gave me the glasses and while I was winding that screw on them so I could see clear he said, "You did me a big favor. I've been looking forward to this fight, but I came down on a late train and by the time I got here there wasn't a ticket to be had. It looks like Abruzzo is a national hero."

I said, "He's a good fighter all right," but I didn't like him to bother me while I was monkeying around with the glasses. Then all of a sudden I was looking right at Al Judge and it was like catching a pail of cold water on my belly. Before I even thought, I jumped right back in my seat so he wouldn't see me. Then I remembered I was looking through the glasses and he couldn't see me at all. I was scared for a minute I wouldn't find him again, but it was easy now that I knew where he was.

He was sitting with a little typewriter in front of him and he was half turned around to say something to the man by the bell. His overcoat was off, but the big white scarf hung loose around his neck, and over the back of the chair was the cane. It was Al Judge all right, and I had him pinned down. He couldn't walk fast with his bad leg, I figured, and before he could get up from the chair I would be downstairs and right behind him.

Then the redheaded man said, "What's so interesting?" and started to reach for the glasses, and I gave them back before he could see where I was pointing them.

I said, "I saw my friend down there," and he said, "Hell, the way you jumped I thought it was some good-looking babe taking her clothes off."

Then he stuck his hand out again and said, "The name is Cooper. Dr. Lloyd Cooper. What's yours?" and I shook his hand and said, "George LaMain."

I was sorry right away. If there was going to be any trouble about what I did to Al Judge, it would be that much easier to put the finger on me. I mean, somebody knowing my name was bad and I started to sweat about it. Then I got an idea and I said, "I got a bet on with my friend, and if you're a doctor maybe you can settle it. I bet that a doctor has to keep everything a secret like a priest. Is that true?"

He thought it was a big joke. He laughed and said, "Not my kind of doctor. I'm a Ph. D."

"What kind is that?"

"That's the kind that knows a lot about nothing. I'm a college instructor. Teach at Troy College upstate. Even so, I think you win the bet about doctors and secrets."

I didn't win any bet, because if he wasn't a real doctor I shouldn't have said my name, but I was wondering if he wasn't lying about it. We have a doctor comes in the bar now and then and we have to call him mister because if the guys hear he's a doctor they start to bother him about what they have, and he doesn't like that. I figured maybe Dr. Cooper didn't want me to ask him stuff about being sick and doctors, and that's why he said he was only a college professor. He didn't look like a college professor either. I mean he was young and pretty sharp, and they're all kind of old, I figured. I took a quick look at him, but he saw me and said, "What's the matter? Something worrying you?"

I said, "What do you teach?"

"Oh, that. I'm preparing a load of foreign correspondents for shipment to the big city. I'm in the English department. Specialize in journalism."

When he said that, the first thing I thought was crazy. I knew it but I couldn't stop it buzzing through my head. I thought, Al Judge knew everything about me and this guy was a friend of his he got to tail me, and I was a sure goner. Almost before I knew it, I turned a little sideways on the seat and got my hand on the gun. Then I knew it was crazy, it was too much of a long shot, and I started to breathe all right again. But even if it was a long shot, I had to make sure. I read plenty books and stuff where you find out what happens to guys who get careless. So I kept my hand on the gun and I said, "Do you know Al Judge?" I watched his face while I said it.

"You mean the *Press* sports editor?"

"Yes. Do you know him?"

"Christ almighty, he was the first man I worked for when I got out of journalism school! And if there was ever a better excuse for getting out of newspaper work, I never found it."

He wasn't lying. I was watching his face, and he meant it. Then he said, "Maybe I shouldn't have talked like that. Is he a friend of yours?"

I said, "No," and then I sat up straight and let go of the gun because there was a lot of excitement downstairs with everybody yelling and some guys whistling and Rocks Abruzzo came into the ring, and right after that Joe Shotfield came in the other side.

After Dr. Cooper was done looking through the glasses, I looked through them and I could see both of them very clear. But mostly I wanted to look at Al Judge, and when I got the glasses on him he was banging away at the typewriter and the scarf was flapping around right by his hands and it didn't seem to bother him. After I gave the glasses back, I could see that white scarf no matter where I looked. It was always in the corner of my eye, and I felt good about that.

I thought the fight would start right away now, but

it didn't. There was still a lot of walking around and talking in the ring, and then a man got in the middle and he made some fighters come up and wave their hands at everybody.

All this time Rocks Abruzzo was sitting there, and there were a couple of men talking to him and one of them pointed to Joe Shotfield and Rocks Abruzzo shook his head. Joe Shotfield was tall and kind of skinny and he was holding on to the ropes and jumping up and down. I could see all that even without the glasses.

But it took a long time and I could feel my hands getting colder and colder while I was watching and keeping that white scarf in the corner of my eye. The gun hurt me too. The way I was sitting my pants were pulled tight, and something on the gun was sticking into my leg. I was afraid to move around and fix it because of the way Dr. Cooper was leaning over.

Then all of a sudden Dr. Cooper said, "Why are you so interested in Al Judge anyhow?"

I said the first thing that came to me. "I want him to get me a job."

"On the *Press*? For Christ's sake, that's where the gag started about the guy telling his kids he played piano in a whore house because he didn't want them to know he worked there."

"I don't care. I want to work on a newspaper and maybe he can help me."

"Why Al Judge?"

"He's a big shot. I want to talk to him about it." An idea was really cooking in my head now and I said, "Do you know where he goes after the fights?"

"That wouldn't help you any. You just go to the personnel office of the *Press*, and tell them what you want. They'll make sure you don't get it."

"I have to talk to him about it."

He shook his head and started to say something but I couldn't hear him. The bell had gone off and everybody was yelling because the fight started. And right off Rocks Abruzzo came out and started smacking Joe Shotfield around. He hit him with everything and then they got tangled up together and the referee ran over and pulled them apart and it started all over again. But what bothered me was when they started fighting the lights all went out except over the ring, and it was hard to see that white scarf. I couldn't see it out of the corner of my eye at all. I had to keep looking straight at it, and that's how I knew when the rounds were over. Because then the lights went on and it was easy to see.

Then there was a real riot and I had to look because Rocks Abruzzo got in a good one, the one everybody wanted to see, only I didn't see it, and Joe Shotfield was down and he must have been hurt bad. He couldn't even get up when it was all over. They had to carry him to his corner.

Then I felt with my foot my father's good hat was on the floor, and I picked it up and saw it was dirty all over. I was scared about that and what he would say, and I started to dust it off. Then I remembered the scarf.

I looked down quick and it wasn't there any more. I was so mad that I grabbed the glasses right out of Dr. Cooper's hand, and he looked like I was nuts. But no matter how I looked around with them, I couldn't find that scarf. The typewriter was gone, the cane was gone too, and I knew for sure Al Judge would get away from me if I didn't do something quick to find him.

Then I remembered Dr. Cooper might know where he went to so I grabbed his arm. I said, "Look, it's important. Where does Al Judge go after the fights? I mean, is there any place special? I have to know because he went away already and I have to find him."

"About that job?"

"Yes. I have to get that job. I just have to."

I was starting to get up, but he pulled me back so I was sitting down again. He said, "Is it Al Judge you were looking at through the glasses?"

"I had to know where he was so I could talk to him. Does he go back to the paper now?"

"You ought to polish up your lying, George. First it was your friend; then it was Al Judge. And all you want to do is ask for a job. You don't expect me to believe all that stuff, do you?"

I said, "Honest to God."

"Listen," he said, "I'll tell you what's bothering you. You were working for the *Press*, and Judge had you fired off your job, and now you want to square it somehow, don't you?"

The way I tried to pull my arm loose was a giveaway, but I couldn't help it. All I wanted to do was get away from there and do it quick, but he held my arm so tight I was afraid it would start trouble where everybody would look. Dr. Cooper said, "He's done that to a hundred guys, and the smart ones forget it and shop around for another job. When you tangle with him you're looking for trouble. I once saw him whack a copy boy over the head with his cane for looking at him cross-eyed. What did you expect to do? Beat him up?"

The finger was on me good now. Whatever I did, Dr. Cooper would figure out who it was, and he even knew my name. The only thing to do was get him somewhere and give it to him and that would fix it up. But what about all the people who saw me with Dr. Cooper, and maybe if my picture was in the papers they would put the finger on me for that.

All I wanted to do was kill Al Judge and kill him quick. I didn't want to kill Dr. Cooper, because that would be murder and not like killing Al Judge. I wasn't even sore at Dr. Cooper, only a little because he was getting everything balled up.

Then it hit me I could get Dr. Cooper to help me, and I could do the job so good I would be all right. I would only know that when I did the job, and if it didn't turn out right, there would be time to get Dr. Cooper too.

I said, "That's what happened. What you said."

"What exactly?"

"I was a copy boy and Al Judge didn't like me so he had me fired. Now my whole family is broke."

"I know how you feel. I felt that way myself ten years ago. But it's smarter to forget it."

"I don't care. I want to give him what's coming to him."

We were looking at each other and Dr. Cooper was moving his lips in and out over his teeth like he was thinking hard. He said, "If there was ever anybody who needed a good shellacking, it's Al Judge. But you're not the guy to do it."

"I'll take my chances."

"You mean that no matter what I say, you're bound to do it sooner or later."

"That's right."

There was a fight on in the ring, but we didn't watch it. We were watching each other. Dr. Cooper rubbed his hand around his chin. "I'd like to be there when it happens. And I could find twenty other guys in half an hour who'd back you up."

"I don't want anybody around."

He looked at me worried. "You don't expect to use brass knuckles or a roll of nickels or something like that, do you?"

"No. But I don't want anybody around." He didn't understand if he was around when it happened I would have to get him too. And I didn't want to do that.

He shook his head and laughed. "George, I think you're crazy, but you're a man after my own heart. As a matter of fact, if you can do the job in style, I know three guys in the racket who'll give you jobs tomorrow."

I said, "Then where is he now?"

"If things haven't changed in ten years, he's probably over at Tuffy's, hoisting a couple. You'll never get him alone there, but you can tail him when he goes out until you get him where you want him."

He said it so much like my thoughts that it sounded like an echo coming back to me. I said, "Where would he go after Tuffy's?"

"Well, his story is in, but he might want to do a column on the fight. That means he'd head back to the *Press.*"

"Does he go home after that?" I wanted to ask was he married or maybe living with some people, so I would know how everything stood, but I was afraid it wouldn't sound right.

Dr. Cooper said, "Hell, nothing may be the way I told it. The best bet is to start at Tuffy's and tag along."

"Where's Tuffy's?"

He said, "Right across the street, from the Garden," and then, when I started to push my way out, he grabbed his coat and hat and came right after me. He said, "I hope you don't mind my going part of the way, George. You're making an old dream of mine come true, and I owe you a drink for that."

I wished he hadn't done that. Because the more he followed me, the more he was getting into trouble, and he was so nice it was crazy to think about killing him. I mean, he was a professor and all that, but he cursed like anybody else, and he was being friendly like Flanagan was sometime.

And here he was getting more and more into trouble, and I couldn't even tell him about it. Because the big thing was to kill Al Judge, and that might spoil it.

CHAPTER NINE

I KNEW about the guy who ran Tuffy's. His name was Tuffy Walsh, and ten, twenty years ago he was one of the best fighters around. He was only a little guy but he had plenty of heart and he wasn't afraid of anybody. He even had a fight with the heavyweight champ and he would have licked him but he didn't have enough weight. I knew all this because only a couple of months back there was a big piece in the *Press* about him, and all the old-timers in my father's bar started to argue about it.

The piece said that Tuffy Walsh was all fed up with fighting and drinking and stuff like that and he was writing poetry. It must have been good poetry too, because they were making a book out of it and there was even one of the poems in the *Press*. It told how things looked in the Wintertime when there was snow all over the ground, and it sounded all right to me. A lot of guys think poetry is dumb, but I don't. There's a couple of poems in Rudyard Kipling that are all right, and once I tried to write one but it didn't come out good. So I knew Tuffy Walsh was plenty smart if he could write good poems like the one in the *Press*.

But some of the guys started laughing and said Tuffy Walsh must be punchy from all the fights he had, and that got old Mr. Reardon and Flanagan all hot. Mr. Reardon started telling about the fights Tuffy Walsh had and who he licked, and Flanagan said all the Irish were full of music and poetry and it was nothing to be ashamed of. Then one of the guys said all the Irish were full of —— and there would have been a fight only my father broke it up. But Flanagan went into the toilet with the *True Story* magazine and wouldn't come out for an hour.

When I was standing outside Tuffy's with Dr. Cooper I didn't think about that. The thing on my mind was if I walked into Tuffy's and Al Judge saw me and remembered me, there would be trouble. I didn't know what kind of trouble, just trouble. Because if he made some kind of crack or did something I didn't like, I might pull out the gun in front of everybody and give it to him right there.

Dr. Cooper was half way in the door but I was still outside. He turned around and said, "What's the matter? Losing your nerve?"

I said, "No. But if he sees me there might be trouble right away, and I don't want that to happen."

He said, "Hell, you're the one that's looking for trouble. Come on in and look him in the eye. Besides, I owe you that drink."

I couldn't stand there and argue it out. I followed him into the bar, but I kept my hand tight on the gun and moved it a little to make sure it would slip out easy if I needed it.

The first one I saw inside was Al Judge. There were some guys all along the bar drinking, and then it curved around until it hit the wall, and he was right in the corner by the wall with a drink in one hand and a pencil in the other writing on a piece of paper in front of him. You couldn't miss him the way that white scarf stood out against the black coat, but I had to take a good look before I saw the handle of the cane hanging on the bar.

When we went up to the bar, I couldn't take my eyes off him. Dr. Cooper said, "For Christ sake, the way you're looking at him, I think I'll lay a bet on you. What have you been doing, training on raw meat?"

Then the bartender came over and stood there with his hands resting on the bar and Dr. Cooper said, "What'll it be?"

The way he said it and the way the bartender stood waiting made me feel good. Flanagan said nobody in the world can figure your age better than a bartender because if he makes a mistake they take his license away. Plenty of times I saw him chase away guys who looked like real big stuff only they were really kids, and he was never wrong. So when the bartender was waiting to give me a drink, I knew I would pass all right and that's why I felt so good. And I knew what to say and do too, because when you hang around a bar all the time you pick up all the angles.

I said, "I'll take whatever you do," and Dr. Cooper said to the bartender, "This is an occasion, general. Make it two Metaxas."

That was stuff my father never had, but I didn't want to look dumb so I didn't ask about it. I figured it was brandy because the bartender poured it into brandy glasses, the very little kind, and it must have cost plenty because Dr. Cooper passed over a five-dollar bill and hardly got back any change at all. He picked up the glass and said, "To the Greeks," and started drinking it down slow. I started to do that but I didn't like the taste, so I slugged it all down in one shot.

It was strong all right. For a couple of seconds I couldn't catch my breath, and when I did it felt like my face was on fire and I was hot inside all the way down to my belly. But it wasn't the kind of hot you get from eating bad stuff. It was like all my juice was percolating and I was so strong I could squeeze my hand around the glass and break it into little pieces.

I looked at Al Judge, the way he was writing on that piece of paper, and I started to figure I couldn't wait much longer. If I went over and bumped into him or something he might start trouble and I could give it to him right there. Everybody would see he started it so it would be all right.

Before I could figure it out better, Dr. Cooper said, "How about another one, George?" and I remembered about my ten dollars because it was my turn to treat. I mean, Dr. Cooper gave me the ten dollars for the ticket so he knew I had it on me, but I didn't have it. And I couldn't tell him why not because it would sound dumb.

I didn't know what to say. I started poking my hands around in my pockets even though I knew there was nothing I could find except the nickel, and Dr. Cooper hit me on the back and said, "Listen, George, this is a celebration, and it's on me. Order up and skip the details."

I said, "Well, all right," like I meant to pay only he

talked me out of it, and we had another and this time it went down easier. When I looked in the mirror in back of the bar I could see myself easy because I was almost a head taller than anybody else, and it felt good with the black hat pulled down, and the glass in my hand, and seeing the white scarf out of the corner of my eye and knowing the gun was in my pocket all ready to kill Al Judge. It felt terrific, and I almost laughed the way Al Judge was standing there just waiting for me to give it to him.

Dr. Cooper said, "If I didn't have my lousy job to think about, George, I'd be in there with you all the way. There's a job you have to see before you can appreciate it, George. Thirty characters sitting around waiting for you to turn them into Walter Lippmanns. Thirty Cinderellas, George, and I'm the fairy godmother. Christ!"

I said, "It sounds like a good job. It sounds all right to me."

"Thirty characters. If they had your guts, George, do you know what they'd do? They'd get out and learn it the hard way. That's what I tell them. Get out and be a man!"

He put more money down and he had two right in a row, but this time he slugged them straight down. He thought for a long time and then he said, "Do you know what that Ph. D. cost? Fifteen hundred bucks. A fifteen-hundred-dollar investment. You buy them in Troy instead of life insurance."

I couldn't figure out what he was talking about, but he looked like he wanted me to say something so I said, "Fifteen hundred dollars is a lot of money."

The bartender fixed us both up and we slugged it down together. Then after a while I saw Dr. Cooper was talking. It was like his lips were moving only the words were coming from someplace else. He said, "Take your chances, George. That's what you said, and I'm with you all the way. Just get in there and take those chances."

Everything was pretty rocky then, and I couldn't remember saying anything like that, but I was glad Dr. Cooper felt the way he did about it because then I wouldn't have to get him after I got Al Judge. And when I thought about Al Judge, I turned to look at him, and there was the white scarf and the cane going back through the tables to where there was a men's-room sign.

I was holding on to the bar, and when I let go, my knees were all loose under me. That was the first I knew I was getting drunk, and I was glad I found out in time, because if I kept it up maybe Al Judge would have gotten away altogether. But I wasn't really drunk so it was all right. My mind was working fine and I knew just what I was doing. I knew if Al Judge was alone in the men's room, I could do the job right away and then it would be all over.

I took a good grip on the gun and I walked back between the tables until I came to the men's room. Then I pushed open the door and walked in. It took only one good look to tell I was alone with Al Judge all right.

There was a long mirror on the side where you came in and under it were three sinks to wash your hands. On the opposite side were a couple of booths and a couple of standing places. The cane was hanging over the door of the last booth, and Al Judge was washing his hands in the sink.

My mind was working a mile a minute. When I came in I felt the door and there wasn't any lock I could snap to keep people out, but next to me was a big window that opened on to an alley. If something went wrong, I could be out that window in a second.

I moved so my back was against the window, and I slipped the safety off the gun and started to pull it out of my pocket. All this time he was rubbing soap around his hands and each finger like I saw doctors in the movies when they get ready for an operation or something. He didn't look around at me once.

Then all of a sudden the door swung open and a guy came walking in right over to the middle sink so he stood between me and Al Judge. I hardly got the gun shoved back in my pocket when I saw the guy was the same one who got my ten dollars, and I started to tighten up again, the way I did when he had me pushed back against the radiator.

He pulled up his coat sleeves a little, and then he saw Al Judge and said, "Hello, Al," and Al Judge said, "How's everything, Peck?"

The guy was slopping water all over his hands, not careful like Al Judge but any which way, and then he took a paper towel from the rack and said, "Can't complain. How'd you like the fight?"

Al Judge said, "It stunk," and he got a towel too, and started to dry his hands. All that time I stood by the window and didn't move. I was afraid if I moved, this guy Peck would see me and start trouble. Then Al Judge went out through the door and it happened just the way I was afraid it would. I took one step after him, and this guy got a good look at me and then quick shoved the door shut with his foot so he was standing in front of me with his back to the door. He said, "What is this, bud? Your hangout?"

Maybe Al Judge would hang around the bar some more and maybe he wouldn't, but I couldn't take any chances on it. I reached around Peck for the doorknob, but he had his back jammed tight against it. I said, "Honest, Mr. Peck, I'm not doing anything. I just came in to take a leak and I have to get out quick because I think my friend is waiting."

"My name is Peckinpaugh, bud."

"I didn't know. I heard Mr. Judge call you Peck so I thought that was your name. Please, Mr. Peckinpaugh, I have to see my friend."

He pushed my hand away from the doorknob and said, "Don't shove me around, bud. Don't you know about me? I don't like to have anybody shove me around."

I could see in my mind the way Al Judge was going out of the front door and going away some place where I couldn't find him, and I started to tremble all over. Not from being scared, but just because I was so sore. I tried to grab the doorknob again and I said, "I'm not trying to shove you around. I just want to get out of here."

"I don't like anybody to call me a liar either, bud," he said, and all of a sudden he slammed me right across the face with his hand. "What are you up to, bud? If you're on the level, what are you sweating about?"

I don't remember in all my life anybody ever hit me like that. I was so surprised I just put my hand up there and I could almost feel my cheek swelling up under it.

I yelled, "You got my ten bucks! Isn't that enough! Why don't you let me alone!"

I saw from his face he was mad enough to kill me. He let go of my wrists to grab at the front of my overcoat with both hands, and that was all the chance I needed. Before he had his hands on me I had the gun out. I went back one step and swung the butt against his head as hard as I could: It shows how quick your mind can work, because when I went for the gun I only thought of shooting, but when I got it in my hand, I knew I couldn't take a chance. Everybody in the bar would hear the noise.

The butt of the pistol hit him right in the side of the head over the ear, and it sounded like a melon hitting the sidewalk. It evened us up all right, because he got the kind of surprised look I must have got when he hit me. Then he started to put his hand up there, but before he could do it he went down in a pile right at my feet.

I grabbed hold of him by the collar. First I was going to stick him in one of the booths so it would look like he was there on business, but I was afraid it would take too long. I dragged him over to the window, and managed to hoist him through so he hit the alley with a bump. Then I slammed the window down.

After that I saw I was doing everything with the gun still in my hand, and I put it back in my pocket quick. Then I opened the door and went up to the bar as fast as I could.

Dr. Cooper was there. He was in the same place, talking to a couple of guys with their heads all together and laughing. But no matter how I looked Al Judge was nowhere around.

CHAPTER TEN

When I was a little kid I used to go to church parties at St Theresa, and they had a game called blindman's buff. One kid would have a handkerchief around his eyes so he couldn't see, and the other kids would run around and yell and make noise, and the kid who couldn't see would have to catch one. I didn't like it because my feet were big, and I couldn't get out of the way so good, so I was "it" more than anybody. And then in my head I could see how I must look, bumping around trying to catch somebody, and maybe all the time he was right in back of me. It made me feel dumb.

And when I saw Al Judge was really gone that's how I felt all over again. All I could think was Al Judge knew all the time what I was out for and he was making it into a game and I hated him for it. If he came back through the door then I would have given it to him one, two, three, and not even worried about the trouble it would get me into. I was in plenty of trouble anyhow, what with this guy laying out in the alley, maybe hurt bad, and Dr. Cooper knowing too much about what I was figuring to do.

All I wanted to do was get Al Judge in the right place and let him know what the score was and then kill him, but everything kept getting mixed up with it, like this Peckinpaugh and Dr. Cooper. It was all because of that extra ticket too, because if I didn't have the extra ticket I couldn't sell it to Dr. Cooper and get Peckingpaugh started. But the extra ticket was my father's, so it was his fault for not being along with me. And the only reason he wasn't along was because of what Al Judge did, so no matter how you looked at it, it all came back to Al Judge.

What I had to do was get started after Al Judge again and not hang around in Tuffy's to figure it out, because somebody might find Peckinpaugh any minute. I went over to where Dr. Cooper was talking and laughing with the two men, but before I could say anything he saw me and started waving his hand back and forth in front of my face.

"I know everything, George. Everything. You got him in there. Aha, you rat; this one is for the working class. Bango! One punch and it's all over. How about it, George? Can we take a look at the remains now? One punch, hey, George?"

The way he talked I knew he was pretty drunk, and I was scared he wouldn't even know what I was talking about. I said, "He got away. Now I have to find him again. Where do you think he went?

The two others guys were a little drunk but not as much as Dr. Cooper, and they were listening and looking at me. One of them was a big blond guy, bigger than me even, with sort of loose skin over his face and pockmarks all over it. He said, "Who is this guy?" and Dr. Cooper said, very serious, "Oh, excuse me. Excuse me. This is George LaMain, the surly Rover. Mr. Olsen. Mr. Greenspan."

Mr. Olsen was the big guy and he didn't say anything, just made the okay sign with his fingers, but Mr. Greenspan shook my hand and said, "Don't mind Coop. He's pickled. What was that name again?"

He was a little tubby guy, and he didn't have any hat on, so I could see he was bald just like Flanagan, only with black hair all around the edges instead of white. He looked all right to me so I said, "George LaMain."

He looked up at the ceiling and started rubbing his fingers all over his bald spot. "LaMain. LaMain. Where the hell do I remember that name from? It goes back about twelve, fifteen years."

Dr. Cooper patted me on the chest about ten times and said, "Mr. Greenspan is a reporter for the *Times*. The man with the photographic memory. He remembers everything back to the day Horace Greeley started the paper."

Mr. Greenspan said, "You ought to be ashamed, Professor. Horace Greeley never started the *Times*," and Mr. Olsen said, "He started the *News*."

Dr. Cooper said, "Hell, no. That was Aaron Burr," and they all started laughing together so Dr. Cooper didn't even see the way I was shaking him by the shoulder.

I said, "Look, I have to find Al Judge. He went away from here. Don't you even know where he might go now?"

They all slowed down laughing, and Mr. Olsen said, "What do you want him for? Did the paper send you out for him?"

"No, I just want to find him, that's all. Do you know where he is?"

Dr. Cooper said, "It's important. It's the most important thing in the world. George is going to track him to his lair, then *bango!* the kill. That's why it's important."

The way it sounded made me so mad I forgot all about him being a professor or anything. I yelled, "Why don't you shut up!" and I pushed him as hard as I could up against the bar. It didn't even bother him. He just started laughing, but Mr. Olsen said, "Lay off the rough stuff. What the hell are you so hot about anyhow?"

I said, "I'm not hot. I just want to know where Al Judge is, that's all."

"Why?"

"He had me fired off my job for no reason and I want to get even with him. That's why."

"You're nuts. If there's no reason, why don't you take it up with the Guild?"

Now I was all mixed up. I said, "I just want to get even with him, that's all."

Mr. Greenspan said, "Judge has gone haywire, all right. And you know what? It's all on account of that business with his sister, that's what."

Dr. Cooper said, "Oh, that sister. That lovely, lovely sister. He should have married her ten years ago," and Mr. Greenspan said, "What kind of talk is that? He don't have a wife, who else should he worry about?"

Mr. Olsen said to me, "What the hell. Why don't you call up the *Press* and ask them? If he's going back there, they'll probably know it, and if he ain't, they might give you a tip where to find him."

The way I was talking and all excited I forgot all about my legs and how loose my knees were, but when I started going to the telephone booth, I felt like the floor was all hills and a couple of times they weren't there when I was ready for them. And it was hard looking up the number in the telephone book, too, but I finally got it and dialed. It was a good thing I had that nickel.

After a while somebody said, "Daily Press," and I said, "Is Mr. Judge there, please?"

"Mr. Judge? Sports department?"

I said, "Yes," and then there was a long wait, so I got scared my nickel wouldn't be enough. Then somebody else said, "Sports," and I said, "Is Mr. Judge there?"

The voice said, "No, he's not," and I said, "Well, look, is he coming back tonight? I mean, it's very important."

The guy said, "Hold the wire," and then right away he came back and said, "Yes, do you want to leave a message for him?"

I felt so good I didn't even know what I was saying. I said, "No. It's okay. That's all right," and then I hung up the phone.

I went back to the bar and right off I said to Mr. Greenspan, "He's going back to the office. Do you know how long he'll stay there? When do you think he'll come out?"

Mr. Greenspan was drinking some kind of a highball. He shook his head while he was drinking and said, "I don't like any part of this business."

I said to Mr. Olsen, "When do you think?" and he said, "Hell, he's good for an hour, maybe two hours. An hour sure. Why don't you go over there now and hang around?"

That was all right with me. I didn't know the layout, but if I hung around first, I could find where Al Judge would come out and figure what I had to do. But before I could do anything, Dr. Cooper grabbed my arm and said, "George, what time is it?"

There was a big wall clock I could see easy and I said, "Quarter after twelve," and tried to shake my arm loose, but he hung on so tight I couldn't without maybe hurting him.

He said, "Oh, my God. Two hours and a quarter late. George, my friend, before you close in for the kill, would you do me a favor? A little favor?"

I felt like slamming him up against the bar again, but I only said, "What favor?"

"I should have been at the Domino Club two hours and a quarter ago, George, but I am afraid I will never make it on my heavy, heavy wings. Could you drop me off there on your way to the kill? It is exactly two blocks north."

I didn't want to do it because I had everything figured out and I didn't want to take any more chances, but the way Mr. Olsen was looking at me, I couldn't say no. I said, "Okay, if you hurry up," and right then there was a whole lot of noise and excitement in the back end of the bar.

I turned to look and there was a bunch of guys pushing around the door into the men's room, and the door was open, and more people were going back to look every second.

My stomach turned over because I knew what it was. Peckinpaugh had come to, or maybe somebody found him, and now there was plenty of trouble and I had to get out fast. I grabbed Dr. Cooper with one arm around the shoulders and started to hustle him out of the door so that we almost knocked over some people who were coming in.

When we got outside, he stopped in the middle of the sidewalk and I started to shake him and yell, "Where is this place? Where is this place you want to go?"

It never even struck me that I could have just left him there and gone ahead by myself with what I had to do.

CHAPTER ELEVEN

THAT WAS a crazy walk all right. I finally got out of him that the place was on Sixth and Fifty-second, and that meant we had to go up three blocks to Fifty-second, and then all the way over to Sixth. He must have been good and drunk the way he figured it was only two blocks altogether.

The worst part was when we started crosstown and got around Broadway. It looked like the further away from Eighth Avenue I got, the brighter the lights were, and around Broadway it felt like there was a spotlight in my face no matter how I turned. I was sure now this Peckinpaugh was some kind of plain-clothes cop, maybe a big shot the way he talked with Al Judge, and if he came to and told what I looked like, every cop in New York would be out for me. And if they got me they would beat me up good, because that's what they did to guys who hit a cop. I didn't only read that in stories either, because one time Mr. Shaw down the block came home drunk and he kicked little Bobby Shaw so the kid kept crying. It must have been a bad kick, because Mr. Shaw had done it before but little Bobby never cried the same way.

Anyhow, it bothered Mr. Shaw the way Bobby was crying, so he pulled his pants down and sat him on the hot stove and the way he screamed and Mrs. Shaw was yelling, all the people in the house came running and they called the cops. A couple of radio cops came and Kennealy, and he grabbed Mr. Shaw and started pulling him downstairs when all of a sudden Mr. Shaw socked him a good one and knocked him down. When the two other cops saw that, they got good and mad and threw Mr. Shaw all the way down a flight of stairs so he was hurt pretty bad. But Mr. Reardon and the other guys came in the bar next day and they said that was all right. That was what happened to guys who hit a cop.

So I was in a bad spot all right, with the cops maybe out looking for me, and Dr. Cooper pushing and talking so loud everybody turned around to look at us. I had to keep him on my left side too, so he wouldn't bump up against the gun and maybe start trouble, and that meant he was always pushing into people coming the other way.

After a while the fresh air got to him and he started to sober up. It was so cold and windy now everybody was walking around with their heads down and guys kept their hands on top of their hats, and every now and then a woman would grab at her skirt between her legs because it would flap around all of a sudden and show plenty. By the time we got to the Domino Club, Dr. Cooper was walking all right by himself, and he only had a little trouble going down the two steps to the door.

The thing I liked about the Domino Club when we got inside was it was so dark. I mean really dark like a movie house when you first go in. I could see it wasn't like I figured at all. I always thought night clubs were big and fancy, but the Domino Club was only a room with a few dim blue lights along the walls and a little stage at the other end. On the stage were four or five colored guys and they were playing music so loud it made your ears hurt. After a minute I could see tables along the walls and a row of tables down the middle, and people there listening to the music.

Right near the door was a tiny little bar, lit better than the rest of the place. There were a couple of people drinking, and Dr. Cooper pulled me by the arm over to a girl who was sitting there, and said, "Hello."

The way she looked and the way she talked I knew she was very sore. She said, "Oh, Paul Revere. What did you do? Walk down from Troy?" and Dr. Cooper said, "No, I came by dog sled, but one of the dogs threw a shoe outside of Albany."

She said, "You're very funny. You slay me," and turned around to pick up her drink, but Dr. Cooper pushed me up close to her and said, "As it happens, I ran into an old friend of mine. George LaMain. He's in the newspaper game. He's a man with a mission."

She looked at me and said, "Hello," and I said, "Hello."

Dr. Cooper slapped the girl on the back and said, "This is Tanya Rostina. She's a dancer with a mission. She'll straighten you out, George, because you're a terrorist and you have no discipline. Tanya hates people without discipline, don't you, Tanya?"

Tanya said, "Oh, you slay me," and started drinking her beer. All the time I was thinking. If I went over to the *Press* building and hung around, I would be wide open for the cops. But the way this club was, it was so dark and so full of noise nobody would even know I was around. Al Judge wasn't at the *Press* yet when I called, so I figured I had pretty near an hour to wait and the club was a good place.

The thing I had to watch out for was the time, so I wouldn't miss him. There was a little clock on the shelf in front of me, and it said twenty to one. In the phone book I saw the *Press* was some number on East Fortieth Street, so it wouldn't take me long to get there. If I pulled out at quarter after one, I would hit Al Judge with plenty of time to spare.

He would come out of the door and I would be right behind him with the gun. Then he would go by some dark place like a doorway and I would steer him into it. Then it would be all over.

Meanwhile it was all right where I was. The music was so loud you almost had to yell if you wanted to say something, but it was pretty good music. And it was all right being close up against Tanya the way I was. She wasn't pretty like Frances because her face was kind of thin and she had sort of a big nose. But she had big dark eyes and her hair was black and pulled back tight so it looked smooth and shining.

For all she was so thin she was all there in the front and it felt soft and good when my elbow bumped her there. The only thing I didn't like was when I saw her legs, and they were nice legs except when they got up around the calf they were so big it didn't look natural. It wasn't fat either, because when she moved her legs you could see the muscles knot up in a bunch. But I didn't like it anyhow.

Dr. Cooper said, "How many ahead are you?" and she said, "Oh, stop it. I could smell you when you came in the door."

He got up on the stool the other side of her and said to the bartender, "Three Martell."

Tanya said, "You know I don't touch the stuff," and Dr. Cooper said, "Make that two Martell, general. The lady is in training."

Tanya said, "You slay me. You really do," and Dr. Cooper got a little sore. He said, "Now what the hell is wrong. I've been late before."

"Oh, it's not that. Marion is up in the apartment. She moved back in again this morning."

I couldn't figure what they were talking about, but whatever it was made Dr. Cooper so mad he banged his hand on the counter and her beer glass fell over. It was a good thing it was empty. He yelled, "For Christ sake! Couldn't you tell her to get out, or at least wait until the week-end was over!"

"Get out where? She can't go back to him. He booted her out just the way I warned her he would."

"Hell, I can't blame him. She's enough to drive any man nuts. But why do you have to take the responsibility?"

"Because she's my sister."

"The hell you say. Is that the latest slogan? All support, comrades, for our nympho sisters?"

Tanya said, "Oh, you're a riot. You really are," and Dr. Cooper grabbed up his drink and took it down in one shot. There was one in front of me too, but I didn't want to drink it. I still felt sick inside from the other drinks and my mouth had a funny taste, so I figured I would just let it stand unless somebody noticed it, then I would drink it down. Besides, it felt just as good standing up against Tanya the way she felt when I pushed against her and not even caring. It was the kind of feeling you know is bad but you can't get rid of it. It gets stronger and stronger until you start to think of all crazy things like grabbing her or something. Things you would never do, but you can't get rid of the feeling anyhow.

But nobody notices about my drink. Dr. Cooper just put down his glass and said, "Well, that settles it. I'm getting a hotel room through Sunday night. A double," and Tanya shook her head and said, "Not for me, you aren't."

She sat there turning her empty beer glass around and around in her hands and looking at it. She looked so sad I wished there was something I could say, only I couldn't think of anything.

Dr. Cooper said, "You don't expect me to go over

there with you while she sits around and watches like a harpy?"

"You know that isn't so. We'll have the other room all to ourselves."

"Sure. While she scratches at the door and slavers. Why the hell don't you have her committed?"

The way Tanya yelled you could hear it easy even over that loud music. She was so mad I don't think she cared if anybody heard or not. She yelled, "Why the hell don't you go away and leave me alone! You're not making things any easier!"

That scared Dr. Cooper all right. He grabbed her wrist and said, "Listen, I'm sorry. I take it back. But don't ever talk like that," and Tanya said, "Well, what do you want me to say?"

Dr. Cooper looked at me, and I moved a little away from Tanya. He said, "And we're dragging George right into the middle of a real bourgeois family quarrel. Is that any way to teach him discipline?"

Tanya said, "Oh, you're the original Barnum and Bailey all right," but then she turned to me and said, "I'm sorry, George."

I didn't know what to say. I said, "That's okay," and then, because of the way Dr. Cooper was looking at me, I picked up my drink and slugged it down.

Dr. Cooper said, "Well, how about getting a table?

Terry Angelus is on in five minutes, and you wouldn't want to miss that, would you?"

I didn't know who Terry Angelus was anyhow, and the main thing was I didn't want to get away from that clock. I said, "I have to go away at quarter after one," and Dr. Cooper said, "For what?" Then he said, "Oh hell, the mission. Why don't you forget all about it, George? Save it for a rainy day, and have a good time now."

"I can't. I have to be out of here at quarter after one."

That one drink must have stirred up the others in me, because I was starting to feel far away, right while I talked to him. I mean his lips were moving, but the words seemed to come from some other place, like before. "All right. I'll tell you what. We'll sit down and listen to Terry Angelus and then we'll all pull out. It's only three numbers anyhow. You'll have plenty of time."

He and Tanya got down from the bar stools, and I think that's what mixed me up more than anything. I mean the way Tanya was standing next to me so she was almost pressed against me, and I could smell the perfume from her and maybe a little sweat only it smelled wonderful. Like a dream, wonderful I mean, only it was real and I didn't want to spoil it. I said, "Okay," and we walked in the dark to a table and sat down.

I was scared they would tell me to take off my overcoat, but they didn't. Dr. Cooper put his coat and hat on the empty chair that was left, and I put my hat there too, but I kept the overcoat on because of the gun in my pocket I was afraid would show. It was so hot that I felt dizzy and sick from it, but I didn't want to take any chances.

I didn't know who Terry Angelus was because I don't go in for that kind of stuff like some of the kids on the block. I mean some kids would know all about the bands and the singers and they would talk about it plenty, but I liked to read books better. I liked some music when I heard it on the radio, especially André Kostelanetz, only Terry Angelus wasn't like that. But I liked her all right. She was wonderful.

She was a colored woman, but her face was kind of light-colored and she was beautiful. She had her hair twisted up with a big flower in it, and when she came out everybody started clapping and yelling, "Ladybird! Ladybird!" like that was a pet name, so it took a long time before she could get started. Then the band started to play, only very quiet, and she sang a song.

She didn't sing like other singers, because it was like she didn't care what the band was playing at all. It was like the band was playing one song and she was singing another but it always came out right. It was a sad song about how she lost her lover, and when she was done everybody started to yell and clap like crazy.

It was funny how I felt while she was singing. I felt sad, but all the same I felt big, bigger than anything, and I wanted to pull the gun out of my pocket and show it to Tanya and tell her what I was going to do, only that would have really been crazy. I had to hold in the way I felt, and the only thing I could do, there was a bottle on the table, I had a drink fast.

I had another one while she was singing the other songs and then she went away and everybody was yelling and calling, "Ladybird!" but she didn't come back. I was clapping louder than anybody and yelling, "Ladybird," too, but still she wouldn't come back.

I felt so sad that I was almost crying, but I knew what I would do. I would kill Al Judge and then I could come back and stand up by the table and tell everybody. And Terry Angelus would have to sing songs for me. Any song I picked she would sing and nobody else could pick one. And when I got done picking, I would go along with her to where she lived and she would give me the works because she wanted to.

I put my hand on the gun and started pulling, and I thought I would lay it on the table and say to Dr. Cooper, get out of here or I'll kill you. It's loaded, see. I would show him it was loaded and he would sneak away and then I would grab Tanya but she would like it.

But there were two bottles on the table in my way

so I pushed at them and they went tumbling all over the floor and everybody jumped, so I started laughing. They all jumped so slow it was funny. Like a slow-motion picture.

I was sweating right through and I could smell it, but that was no good because there was something else I couldn't remember. Then I thought I remembered what it was because I had to take a leak bad and that must have been it.

I got up from the table, but I almost fell over it, and Dr. Cooper got up too and grabbed me. There was loud music and he was just moving his lips, but I knew he was my friend and he would help me get to the toilet even if he was a professor.

He was drunk all right, because he grabbed hold of his chair when he started walking, and Tanya was sitting there and laughing. And when we got out, she still looked like she was happy and that made me feel good.

Then they both helped me and we all started out, but I pulled away because I couldn't wait to get outside where there was plenty of fresh air. Anyhow, they stopped and Dr. Cooper was figuring out how to pay the waiter and there was no use waiting. But it was lucky too, because when I got outside there was Terry Angelus standing with a big dog on a leash and he was wetting on the lamp-post there.

Most times I don't like dogs because maybe they'll bite you or something. But I liked this dog because Terry Angelus had him on a leash, and I went up and patted his head, and it felt like rubbing your hand on a carpet. He liked me too all right, because he pushed against me and I almost fell down, so I had to grab Terry Angelus and hold her arm.

She didn't mind. She was smiling and was even more beautiful than when she was singing. I just had to tell her how I felt because that's how it was. I knew I had to and I knew she would like it, and I said, "You're the most wonderful singer in the whole world and you're so beautiful even if you are a nigger," and it was hard to say too, because my lips were so stiff I could hardly move them.

But she was mad the way I was hanging on her arm. She was mad about it all right, because she pulled away all of a sudden so I almost fell down again, and then she spit right where my necktie was showing. I put the back of my hand over it and I could feel the spit, and I felt like crying because she was so mad.

But she would do what I wanted all right, because I had the gun, and I grabbed at it and tried to get my hand on it, but before I could find it, Dr. Cooper and Tanya took hold of me and started walking me down to the curb where there was a taxi waiting and we all got in.

I didn't want to go. I had to show Terry Angelus what the score was, but Dr. Cooper yelled to the taxi-driver about Barrow Street and then he grabbed me so I couldn't pull loose. But I could look around through the back window and I did, and Terry Angelus was still standing there with the big dog, rubbing her hand on her forehead, and it looked like she was crying.

Then the taxi started going real fast so I hit my head against the window, but I didn't care. I was glad, because I knew if she was crying she was sorry for what she did to me, and that made everything okay.

CHAPTER TWELVE

I KNEW where Barrow Street was. It was in Greenwich Village, because sometimes after school I would walk there and look in the bookstores. They had the best bookstores there of anyplace, because you could look around all you wanted and nobody would say anything. They had a lot of old books, too, for ten, twenty cents, and once I bought three books all for fifty cents. They were by Rider Haggard, all about a guy who was in Africa and had all kinds of adventures. They were all right.

A lot of kids said, oh, don't go there, don't go there. There's a lot of crazy guys there want to grab you and give you the works like you were a girl or something, but they didn't scare me any. I looked around plenty, and I never saw even one like that.

So when the taxi stopped in the middle of the block,

I knew where I was even if it was so dark. It was the darkest block I ever saw, because the street light was busted and the light was out and there was hardly any light you could see in the windows all around. It was freezing cold, too, and I was all over sweat, so when the wind hit me it felt like somebody rubbing ice over my skin and my teeth started to chatter. If I'd wanted to I could have stopped them chattering, but it felt so funny I almost laughed.

Then a newspaper came blowing along and almost hit me in the face, and I thought of the paper that blew against Mr. Ehrlich's fence. I knew when that paper stuck there I stopped being a kid, and as long as it stayed that way I was big stuff and I could do just what I wanted. Only I was scared, because if it blew away again I would have to go back to being a kid again, and didn't want to.

I knew what to do about that all right. When I got back home I would take a hammer and nails and nail it right into the fence so it could never blow away again. And if Mr. Ehrlich or somebody tried to take it away, I would pull out the gun and let them have it. I would kill anybody who tried to take that paper away. It would be too bad for them if they tried it.

When we got into the house it was nice and warm, and there was a lot of stairs. I could walk up the stairs all right. If I wanted to I could go up four steps at one time, only Tanya said, "Shh," and I didn't want to make her sad again so I went up the regular way. But it wasn't any good her saying, "Shh," like that, because the more we went up, the more I heard some music coming real loud out into the hall. I wasn't the only one either, because Dr. Cooper said, "That sounds like your sister all right," and Tanya said, "Goddammit. She'll be having me thrown out of here," and started running very fast up the steps.

Outside the door she had trouble looking for her key, and while I was standing there I could hear the music close up and it sounded terrific. It was real heavy stuff, and it would start out like nothing much and then all of a sudden it would open up like thunder and go right over me. Then Tanya got the door open and she ran right in and turned off the music. I wished she hadn't done it, because it was wonderful.

It was a big room there without any carpet at all, not even linoleum. Just plain bare wood. And books all around. More books than I ever saw anyplace except the bookstore. There were so many they were even piled up on the floor. And there were piles of phonograph records too.

There was a couch up against the opposite wall between the windows and it was made up like a bed, the way mine was. And there was a girl sitting on the couch in her pajamas, only not a girl really because she wasn't so young any more. She looked more like a schoolteacher, sort of. She had black hair like Tanya, but it was cut straight across in bangs the way little kids have it, and her face was thin with a big nose like Tanya too, but the rest of her was so skinny it was flat all the way down. You could see that easy through the pajamas, and you could see the way her hands and feet were skinny too.

She looked kind of sick to me. Her face was white and she had on sort of thick, shiny lipstick, almost purple, so it made her face look even whiter. When we came in, she was looking at a book, then she quick grabbed a piece of Kleenex out of a box on a little table in front of her and started to rub away at her nose. The way it was so red and the way her eyes were so shiny, I figured maybe she was crying about something, and that made me feel bad.

Tanya switched off the music and then walked over to the little table. There was a bottle on it with some white pills and Tanya grabbed it up and looked at it like she was good and sore. Then she shoved it into her pocket and said, "If you aren't impossible."

The way it looked, the girl didn't even hear what Tanya said. She kept looking at me in such a funny way, and she said, "Hello. Are you one of Lloyd's students?"

Dr. Cooper said, "Student, hell. This is George La-Main, the crusading journalist. George, this is Marion Gordon, Tanya's sister. She's a poet without peer or periodical," and Tanya said, "Don't strain yourself, Lloyd."

The way Marion was leaning forward and looking at me made me feel all prickly in my stomach. She said, "Do you like poetry, George? Really like it?" and I said, "Sure. I liked that music too. What was that?"

"What?"

I said, "That music you were playing when we came in. It was all right."

"Oh, that was the Sibelius First. Did you really like it? Shall I play it again?"

I said, "Sure," but Tanya said, "Oh no you don't. Just sit nice and quiet while I get the drinks. And take off your hat and coat, George."

She went into the kitchen, and I pulled off the overcoat and my hat, and I put them on a chair that was standing empty. Then I sat down in an armchair and I felt the gun push into my leg. It didn't matter if they saw it or not, but it was better that they didn't. So when I sat down, I turned a little sideways and made believe I was getting set right, but meanwhile I slid the gun out and shoved it under the chair cushion.

It must have looked a little funny because Dr. Cooper said, "Hunting for buried treasure, George?" but I only said, "No. I want to get set right." I felt like pulling out the gun and showing it to him so he would know who he was fooling around with, but maybe that would scare Marion, and I didn't want her to stop looking at me the way she was.

She said, "You know, you've got a very striking face, George. It's youthful but very strong," and I liked that too. The way she said it and the way she looked at me, my mind was going all around thinking if only Tanya and Dr. Cooper would go away something big would happen. She hardly had any clothes on either, and it would be so easy I could see it all the way I would do it. I wouldn't kiss her because of the way she looked, but I would do everything else and find out all about it.

Then Tanya came in with a bottle of wine and some glasses and said, "This is just some stuff we had around but it'll have to do," and we all had some. It was sour but plenty strong, and when it got down it warmed me all through again and somehow got mixed up with what I was thinking about Marion, so I could feel the prickling all down my belly into my private business and the blood going so hard in me it sounded like a drum thumping in my ears.

It got worse and worse too, because Tanya came

around with the wine until it was all gone and then she sat down on Dr. Cooper's lap, and Marion got a skinny little book with poems in it or something and she started to read it but I couldn't hear what she was saying. I kept looking at Tanya and Dr. Cooper and watching what they were doing, and all I could think of was I wanted to do it with Marion but she might not want me to and there would be trouble.

Then Tanya got another bottle of wine, but a new one, so Dr. Cooper opened it up and a lot spilled all over and it made me feel sick when I saw it. I don't know why, but when I saw it splashed all over the floor and running in the cracks of the wood I had to cry. I didn't care, I just cried in front of everybody and Tanya gave me more wine and said something but I couldn't hear what.

Marion just sat and read poetry, and all I could see was her eyes and her lips moving and I knew it was crazy but I thought maybe there's nothing left of her only lips and eyes, so even if she let me do something it wouldn't be any good.

Then it was hard to see anything, and I looked around and Tanya and Dr. Cooper weren't there any more and Marion was standing by the lamp next to the couch and there was only a little light in it so you could hardly see. And I knew the way she was standing there and looking at me she wouldn't mind what I wanted to do, and then I got scared.

I wouldn't know how to do it right. I never did it before. I didn't know anything about how it really was, so I would spoil everything and she would see I was only a dumb kid and they would all laugh at me.

She was standing by the couch just looking at me and I could see the light shining on her lips. I put my hand under the chair cushion and took hold of the gun. If they laughed at me I would give it to them. I would give it to Dr. Cooper first, and then I would make Marion take off her pajamas and I would make Tanya take all her clothes off and I would do plenty to them. I would beat them with a cane on their back until they were all stripes like a purple rope and then they would fall over on their backs and I would shoot them in their private business. Right where it hurts.

She came away from the lamp and started walking to me. It was hard getting up, but I did it with the gun in my hand behind me waiting for her to laugh. But she didn't laugh. She didn't say anything, only went to the phonograph, and then I heard that music start up again but not loud this time. Just loud enough to hear.

It was crazy, that music. It was like me trying to get up my nerve to do something, and then all of a sudden coming out with it like a big wave that goes crash on the beach. Then Marion was up against me, and I dropped the gun back on the chair and grabbed her as tight as I could.

I didn't have to worry about her laughing. I didn't have to worry about anybody laughing. She knew everything and she showed it all to me, and it was more wonderful than I ever dreamed in my best dreams.

CHAPTER THIRTEEN

FIRST WHEN the noise came through to me I didn't think about it. I just lay there remembering about Marion and me and what it felt like and how I could do it again whenever I wanted. I could do it with her because of the way she liked me, but I could even do it with other girls now that I knew what it was all about.

That was the most important thing in the world, and when you had it everything else was kid stuff. Even school and books didn't matter then, because you knew all about the real thing and you weren't a kid any more. It felt so good thinking about it that I didn't want to stop, but the noise got louder and louder and I got all tangled up in my mind.

I figured it was the clock. The clock behind the bar at the Domino Club was ticking louder and louder because it was pretty near quarter after one and I had to go find Al Judge.

Then I opened my eyes quick because I knew it couldn't be the Domino Club. It was freezing cold in the room, and I was laying half off the couch without any clothes so I was shaking all over, and the noise was the needle on the record going around and around the way it does when the music is over and you don't stop the record.

The little light in the lamp was still on so I could see what I was doing. I got off the couch and went over to the phonograph careful so I wouldn't fall over, and hunted around until I switched it off. There were clothes all around the floor and I started to put my stuff on quick before Marion would see me. She was sound asleep on her back with the blanket up to her chin, and her mouth open with the lipstick smeared all around it, but I felt ashamed until I got some clothes on.

Then all of a sudden it hit me what time it must be and I got scared. I turned the big light on in the lamp so I could see better and then I looked all around the room for a clock, but I couldn't find one.

Then I really got scared. If Al Judge was already gone from the *Press* maybe I would have trouble finding him again, and before I could the cops might be on me for what I did to Peckinpaugh. I found the gun on the armchair and I put it into my pocket. Then I went over to Marion and started shaking her hard. First she just moved her head like the light was bothering her, then she opened her eyes and looked at me.

"What's the matter?"

I said, "What time is it? I have to find out what time it is!"

She started sitting up with the blanket held up against her, and then she lay down again and said, "It doesn't matter. Tanya doesn't mind."

I didn't know what she was talking about. I grabbed her shoulder and started shaking it again. "I have to know what time it is, don't you understand? Don't you have a clock?"

This time she sat all the way up. She held up the blanket with one hand and starting slicking down her hair with the other. "There's a clock in the kitchen. Do you have to go to work now?"

I didn't bother to answer her. I ran into the kitchen and the light cord bumped my face. I grabbed it and turned on the light. There was a refrigerator in the corner, and on top of it was a big alarm clock. I looked at it and thought I was crazy. It said four o'clock. I looked at it close. I even picked it up and listened so I could hear it ticking, and when I looked at it again it still said four o'clock.

There was a cupboard right next to the refrigerator, and a telephone was on it. I took hold of the phone, but I couldn't think of the number of the *Press*. Then I started shoving everything around looking for a phone book, but I couldn't find one. I made a lot of noise and Marion came in. She had the pajamas on again, but she had a blanket around her too, because it was so cold. Only she forgot to fix her lipstick, so it was like a clown's mouth.

She said, "What's the matter? What are you doing?"

I said, "I need the phone book. Don't you even have a phone book?"

It was the first time I saw her face real good, the way the kitchen light was shining on it, and it was all like dough, and a smeared mouth, and stupid. It made me sick to think how I had kissed her, and everything, and how she was so dumb she didn't even know where the telephone book was. She kept shaking her head. "I don't know. It must be somewhere around," and looking about like she expected it to come flying up to her. She looked like she was drunk.

The way the clock kept going turned my stomach upside down. It was burning like fire anyhow, and my mouth tasted so sour and dry, I felt I could drink a gallon of water. But if I got out I would find some place with a phone book and I could call from there, so I didn't have time to hang around. I pushed Marion away and went into the other room. I stuck the hat on my head and started getting into the overcoat, and Marion came running in. There was a wad of Kleenex in her pajama pocket and she pulled it out and started to rub all around her nose with it. She said, "Have I done something? What are you carrying on like this for?"

"I don't have the number. I have to call up, but I don't have the number."

I was already at the door when she said, "Why don't you ask Information? Won't they have the number?"

Before she finished saying it, I ran back to the phone. I dialed four-one-one for Information, and all the while I was doing that and then calling the number they gave me, the clock kept going, and Marion kept rubbing her nose with the Kleenex so that I wanted to tell her to take the clock and get away from me.

Then somebody said "Daily Press," and I held the phone tight and said, "I have to know if Al Judge is there. Can I talk to somebody who could tell me?"

Then a guy's voice said very loud, "Sports," and I told him all over again what I wanted.

He said, "Mr. Judge left here an hour ago. Is there any message?"

The only thing that worries me was this guy would hang up, and I had to think of something quick. I said,

"Yes, I have a message for him, I have to give it to him right away. It's very important. Could you tell me where he lives?"

"What do you mean, important? Can't it wait until he gets in tomorrow?"

I yelled, "No! It's important, don't you understand?" And then I remembered Dr. Cooper and Mr. Greenspan and what they were talking about and I said, "It's about his sister."

The guy said, "Oh," and from the way he said it I knew I was on the right track. I said again. "It's about his sister and I have to tell him right away. Just tell me where he lives and I'll go over there right away."

He said, "Hold the line," and then it sounded like there were three or four guys talking right near the phone only I couldn't hear what they said. It took so long that I started to say, "Hello, hello," into the phone when I heard the guy again. "Look, he's not home now. As a matter of fact, he's probably over at her place, but I'm not sure. You want to take a chance?"

I said, "Sure. Sure. Only what's the address?"

"Here it is. West Twenty-eight Street. Two-ninety-nine. Have you got that?"

I said it back to him to make sure and he said, "That's it. But look, what's going on? Can you give us the tip-off?"

I said, "No. I have to tell him," and then I hung up quick. I shoved my hand into my pocket to make sure the gun was okay, and I got that same feeling that my mind was working so it would figure everything out just right and my muscles were like iron. I had to pull my hand away quick though, because Marion pushed up against me and said, "Now you're not upset any more, are you?" and I said, "No. It's okay."

Then I remembered I didn't have any money at all, and it would take too long to walk all the way to Al Judge's sister. I said, "Look, I don't have any money. Could you lend me some? I'll pay it back the next time I come here."

That shows how it is when you stop being a kid, because she didn't ask me about coming again, but I figured it would be all right if I came even without her asking. That was the way the big guys did it, all right.

She went into the parlor and started hunting around and then she found a pocket-book. All I figured on was a dime or maybe a quarter, but she pulled out a bill and pushed it into my hand. I was so surprised I couldn't think of what to say. I just said, "That's okay," and I started to go to the door.

She grabbed hold of my coat sleeve. "But you will be back, won't you?"

I was afraid she might get worried about giving me

all that money and ask for it back, so I said, "Sure. I'll be back tomorrow night. I'll pay you back right away."

She still hung on to my arm. "Don't you even want to kiss me good-bye?"

The way it felt with the gun digging into my leg, and knowing where Al Judge was, it didn't bother me any more, even with that smeared-up mouth. I gave her a kiss and she hung on until I started to feel funny again. Then I pulled away and went to the door. She opened it up for me, and when I was out in the hall, she said, "I'll be expecting you soon," and stood there watching me while I ran down the stairs.

Before I went out the front door into the street I took a quick look at the bill and I knew why she said that. It wasn't a single. It was a five-dollar bill, and she was letting me know, only in a nice way, that I was supposed to pay it back right away.

She was all right. Even with that doughface, and that smeared mouth, and that funny way of looking at you, she was all right.

CHAPTER FOURTEEN

YOU KNOW the best thing Kipling wrote? It was about the English Army that got scared in India and started running away from the enemy. But there were two kids, not even real soldiers because all they did was play a fife and drum, and what do they do but turn around and start walking toward the enemy. Just marching that way toward the enemy all alone, and playing away like crazy on a fife and drum. It was so brave that all the soldiers from both armies just stopped and looked.

That's how I felt. Walking down that black street with the wind roaring away in my ears, I felt like everybody was watching me. My father, and everybody who saw what Al Judge did to him, and Marion, the way she was standing by the door and watching me go down the stairs, they were all standing around the big empty field and waiting for me to go out all alone and finish the job.

They would all know. Maybe not in so many words so I would get in trouble for it, but they would know anyhow. You look somebody in the eye and say, "Isn't it funny what happened to Al Judge," and they put two and two together right away. Then when you walk down the block or go into the candy store and they start whispering together, you know they aren't talking about being yellow or laying down. They're saying you're big stuff all right, but they wouldn't like to get in any trouble with you because you know how to even things up.

Every step I took, that music like waves went through me. I felt so wonderful and strong I wanted to yell as loud as I could into the wind. There was nothing around anywhere except a cat coming out of an alley onto the sidewalk in front of me.

Then I let out a real yell. It wasn't a cat at all. It was a big rat, bigger than any rat I ever saw in the bar, and it was flat on its belly with its whiskers twitching while it looked at me. The way I yelled scared it, and it took off like a black streak across the gutter, and right behind it out of the alley three or four more came running almost over my shoe.

I wasn't scared of them. I chased them all the way across the gutter yelling at them until they ran down into a basement on the other side, and I had to grab the lamp-post with the busted light in it because I almost fell over. I got mad at myself while I was hanging on to the lamp-post. If I used my head I could have pulled out the gun quick and shot a couple of them, but I forgot about the gun.

When I got down to the avenue, there was more light and a couple of people and some cars going by. I had enough money for a taxi, so I went out into the middle of the gutter and started waving my arms and yelling at the taxis when they went by. Only none of them was empty. There was always somebody riding in them, and the drivers would just yell back at me and swing around so as not to hit me.

I didn't have time to hang around any more, the way that music was banging away now and everybody was waiting for me. There was a subway on the corner, and I went down the stairs very careful and over to the change booth. An old guy with white hair sat inside on a high stool reading a paper. When I pushed the five-dollar bill in, he took a look at it and made a sour face. Then he put his face to the opening in the window and said, "Can't you read?" and pointed up at a sign there.

It was the one about how he didn't have to change anything bigger than a two-dollar bill, but way down in the tunnel I heard a noise like the train coming and I didn't have time to monkey around. I shoved the money at him and yelled "Give me my change! Don't you hear the train coming?"

The way Marion gave me the money because she was being nice and this crazy old guy didn't want to take it made me so mad I started to bang the sign with my hand as hard as I could. The guy pushed my money back again. Then he pulled a little gate shut across the bottom of the window and yelled, "Get out of here, you stew bum! Go on, get out of here!"

Then the train came tearing in and I didn't waste any time. I grabbed my money and ran over to the turnstile and jumped over it. The next thing I knew, the gun came tumbling out of my pocket all over the floor and I had to bend down and pick it up.

The old guy had plenty of heart all right. When I went over the turnstile he yelled through the window, "Hey, you! Hey, you!" and then he pulled open the door of the booth and ran out. I grabbed the gun up and pointed it at him and he froze up against the wall next to the booth with his mouth open. Then I turned around and dived into the train just as the door was closing. I put the gun away and looked through the window at him. He was standing at the turnstile, shaking his fist at me and yelling something but I couldn't hear what. Then we went into the tunnel.

The only people in the car were a colored guy and his girl friend sleeping all over each other, but I stayed out on the platform anyhow. The door was open between cars, and you could hear the train crashing back and forth and the chains creaking and the air come rushing in at you and it was exciting. If you knew how, you could stand all right without holding, like on a ship, and I tried to do it but fell up against the door. Then the conductor came across between the cars and slammed the door shut, and it got quiet all of a sudden. He came over to me and said, "What was the trouble? What happened back there?"

He must have thought maybe I stuck up the old guy, the way it looked, and it was so funny I started laughing. I said, "He got mad because I gave him a five-dollar bill to change," and the conductor said, "For Christ sake, the old crank," then it was Fourteenth Street and he had to open the doors.

But he was all right, that conductor. After the train started he came back again and said, "I hope you told him plenty. Too many of these guys get away with murder," and I thought that was so funny, I started laughing all over again only I couldn't tell him why.

Then he said, "Where do you want to get off?" and I told him, "Twenty-eighth Street," and he said, "All right, I'll give you a call."

When he went away, he shut the door behind him but I opened it up again so I could hear the noise better. There were a couple more people in the car now and they looked at me sore because they didn't like it but I didn't care. The train was crashing just like that music and it sounded good to me. And I was getting close to Al Judge, so everything could be finished up and paid off.

Then the conductor yelled down the car, "Twenty-eight," and I got off the train. The noise and the shaking up made me a little dizzy so that the floor was waving under my feet, and it was hard going up the stairs. And my mouth and throat were so dry and swollen it was hard to swallow. It tired me climbing those stairs too, and when I got to the top I had to stop and rest. It shows how I wasn't used to staying out late.

I knew my way around all right. I had to cross the street and go down one block, and the house I wanted would be near the corner of Eighth Avenue. It was as empty and dead here as it was on Marion's block. It wasn't real at all. The way the houses were all dark and quiet and the street was stretching straight out ahead of me with a light shining at the other end, it was like walking down a long black tunnel and the light was where I would come out. It was like a dream I had once.

Just like a dream I had so it felt like I was doing something I did before and the whole thing wasn't real.

I walked slow. I wasn't scared, but that seemed like the right way to do it. Now and then I could make out the number of a house. Two-twenty-seven. Two-fifty-three. And when I saw two-ninety-nine, I put my hand into my pocket and took hold of the gun as tight as I could.

I knew number two-ninety-nine all right. I was in that house plenty times before, and I knew what it looked like and who lived there.

That was the house where Frances lived. There were four apartments in that house altogether, and nobody named Judge lived there. But Al Judge beat up my father and then he came to the house where Frances lived and that's where I would find him. Right with Frances.

It wasn't my fault I didn't have that figured out before, because I never knew the number of the house. It's the same if you asked me where Marion lived. I didn't know the number, but I would know how to get there all right. So it wasn't my fault at all if I didn't know Frances figured in until I was in front of the house.

But it didn't make any difference. Al Judge had it coming to him, and if Frances was there she would get it too. No matter how I looked at it she had it coming to her too, and anyhow she was the kind who would go right to the cops when she saw me kill Al Judge.

I went into the hall and took the gun out of my pocket. There were four doorbells, and Sedziaski was the last name, but I was too smart to push that one. I pushed one of the other buttons for the second floor and waited.

It took a long time. Then the buzzer started going on the door and I pushed it open. The inside hall was all dark and I had to stand still before I could see again. Upstairs, somebody leaned over the banister and called. "Who is it? Who it that?" but it didn't bother me any. Frances lived on the bottom floor, the first door to the right, and I ducked over to the door.

It wasn't closed tight. It was open a crack and there was a light shining through and hitting the wall behind me like a thin yellow line. I didn't stall. I pushed open the door quick, stepped inside, and slammed it shut. It was a good thing I had the gun all ready and aimed. Sitting and looking at me from behind the little table in the middle of the room was Al Judge.

There was a pile of letters and papers and stuff all around him. He must have been reading them when I walked in. His overcoat was thrown over a chair, but his scarf was still hanging loose around his neck.

His cane was there too. It was laying across the table

with the handle a foot away from his hand. I wanted to tell him to throw it on the floor but I didn't want him to get hold of it, and I didn't want to get near and do it myself. I just stood there and kept the gun pointed at him. My finger was so tight on the trigger all he had to do was wink his eyes and the bullet would tear him wide open.

Frances wasn't around. The whole apartment was only one room with a kitchenette on one wall and the closet and bathroom on the other side. The bathroom door was open, and it was easy to see nobody was there.

I just stood there and felt good the way Al Judge was looking at me. Sitting there, he didn't look big any more. Just fat. Like a frog sitting there. And he had a big lower lip that stuck out too, like a frog. First he didn't move a muscle, but started licking his lips as if they had gone all dry on him. Then he moved his hand an inch towards the cane, and I said, "No," and he froze up again.

I knew how he felt when he was looking at my father across the bar. I could have stayed that way an hour, just watching him and waiting to see what he would do. But he didn't hold out long. He wet his lips again and said, "Listen. If you were worried about me talking, forget it. They won't need me."

He was all balled up about it, but he was going to figure it out for himself. And he was going to sweat plenty before I gave it to him. It hit me how the sweat would feel rolling down those stripes on my father's back, and my finger moved so that without my thinking it was nearly all over before he knew what the score was. That was what I had to be careful of.

I said, "I'm not worried about you talking. I like to hear you talk."

"You don't get it, fellow. Peckinpaugh turned in a description of you a mile long when he came to. I don't have a thing to do with it. Not a thing."

That surprised me, because I wasn't thinking about Peckinpaugh, and it must have showed on my face. Al Judge said very quick. "Weren't you laying for Peckinpaugh?"

"No."

"Listen, I'm on the level. A blind man could have seen the way you were laying for him in that toilet. It wasn't my fault I was there."

"I wasn't laying for him."

"You *weren't*?"

"No."

"Then what . . ." He leaned forward with his eyes squinting so you could hardly see them. "Me?"

"Yes."

"What is this? A gag?"

"No. What do you know about Frances Sedziaski? What are you doing here?"

He grabbed the sides of the table and pulled himself up a little. "What the hell is it your business?"

I shoved the gun out at him. "Sit still! I'll kill you if you don't sit still!"

He froze like that, shaking his head from side to side. "Don't go waving that damn gun around, son. You're not in any shape to fool around like that. Just keep your head, and let's talk sensibly."

I liked that. If I wanted, I could make him get down on his hands and knees while he talked to me. He was a real big shot, but if I said the word he would crawl over, bad leg and all, and lick my shoes. He knew how my father felt all right.

I said, "How did you know Frances?"

"Christ! She was my sister."

"Your sister!"

"I'm just going through her stuff. I'm supposed to have it out of here tomorrow."

Now I was all balled up. "Out of here? What for? Where is she?"

"Son, you're too jumpy to handle that gun right. Put it away, will you, and I'll tell you anything you want to know."

"Where is she? What happened to her?"

"Now don't be surprised. I'll tell you, but for Christ sake, don't be surprised. She's been dead a week."

I could hardly keep the gun where it was. I tried to talk but the words didn't come out clear. Al Judge said, "What?"

"Does my father know that?"

"Your father? Who's your father?"

"You know him. Andy LaMain."

He was on his feet so fast I didn't have a chance to tell him not to. "LaMain? He sent you here?"

"Sit down!"

He didn't. He stood there acting crazy. Smiling at me like he wanted to be friends. "Look. Whatever he wants, just help yourself. It's all right with me. What is it? Some letters? I'll help you find them."

He started shuffling through the stuff on the desk with his hands right near the cane and I yelled, "Stop it!"

He stood that way.

I said, "He didn't send me. He doesn't even know I'm here."

The smile went away, and he started shaking his head again very slow. "I don't get it, son. I'm supposed to be smart, but I don't get it at all."

"You're not smart. If I told you to take off your shirt and show me some skin, would you get it?"

He was sweating all over his forehead so you could see the drops shining under the light. He whispered, "You don't understand at all, son. I can see you don't understand. Just let me explain it, so you can get the picture."

He knew the score and he was sweating, and there was no sense waiting any more. There was sweat running down my face too because I could feel it burning my lips. He was looking at me, and he must have known from the way I was inching the gun up what I was going to do. He must have known because for all his fat and that bad leg, he moved faster than anybody I ever saw.

The cane was up in the air so that it looked like a telephone pole was going to fall on me. And under it his mouth was wide open, and his eyes popping, and his face all shining with sweat. It's funny the way he looked like a statue there, and the gun barrel pointing into the middle of his face was like a cannon in front of me.

Nothing happened, everything froze like that, and then all of a sudden there was a little trickle of smoke coming out of the gun, and it was pointing up at the ceiling. Then the whole room smelled bad from smoke and my arm pained me right up to the elbow.

And Al Judge was lying on his side with the cane

under him so all that showed was the handle, and blood dripping down across his face and on to the white scarf.

CHAPTER FIFTEEN

I THINK I was the only one in that whole house who didn't hear the shot. Somebody came galloping down the stairs yelling, "What is it? What's the matter down there?" and then the door to the back apartment went flying open so hard it shook the house, and somebody there started yelling to the one on the stairs, "Did you hear that? What was that?" All that time I felt I was in a dream and trying to fight my way out of it.

It's no good when you kill somebody, even if he has it coming to him. Everybody wants to grab you, and the cops are out for you and it's like a dog running down the street with the kids throwing rocks at him. That's why it was like a dream, only in a dream you can wake up, but this was real.

The thing that started me going again was the way

my hand and arm felt. I knew about guns kicking, but I never knew it was like that. The palm of my hand was already swelling up, and my arm felt like somebody had slammed my funny bone. I could hardly bend it to get the gun in my pocket.

There was no use trying to get out the front way with everybody piling out into the hall. I ran across the room, grabbed the window, and tried to push it up. But it was a ground-floor window, so it had one of those extra locks on it, the kind you have to turn like a screw to loosen up. It was stuck so tight I couldn't budge it. I had it with both hands trying to loosen it up when somebody started banging on the door and yelling, "Hey, in there! What's the trouble in there?"

If I had something to shove into that window lock, I could pry it open, like with a lever. I let go and started looking around the room. Then the knob on the door rattled, and the door began opening. I was near the closet. I pulled open the door, dived in, and pulled the door closed, but not all the way, so it wouldn't click.

It was a wide, shallow closet with a bar running all across it, and a lot of dresses and nurse's uniforms hanging there. There wasn't any room for me to stand, so I got down on my knees and held one hand on the doorknob. If anybody tried to open the door, I could pull it shut and maybe scare them away.

For a couple of seconds it was quiet, and then all of a sudden a woman started screaming so loud I almost slammed the door shut. "Look at that! Look at that! It was a crook, and he's killed him! Look at that!" and a man yelled, "Quiet! Quiet! Do you hear? It's all right!"

She yelled, "Blessed Jesus! It might have been you! I told you not to answer that bell. You could have been dead this minute. Ahhh," and then she started laughing and crying all mixed up, and it sounded like she went crazy.

I had to see what was happening. There was a little crack of light coming through the door, and I put my eye there and looked out. The one who was yelling was a big fat woman with a dirty old bathrobe on and her nightgown coming all the way down to her feet. She had her head back and it was rocking around, and her gray hair was loose and hung down to the middle of her back. She looked like she was ready to fall over, and there was a tall skinny guy trying to hold her. He had on winter underwear with a bathrobe over it too, and he was so mad it looked like he wanted to hit her.

There was another old woman too, a little dried-up one with her cheeks all pulled in so she couldn't have had any teeth, and she had hold of the fat one's hand and was rubbing away at it and slapping it. In back of them was another guy, I guess the dried-up one's husband, with his pants on over his pajamas, and he was pulling and hauling at the cover on the bed trying to get it off. Finally he got it loose, and he ran over and threw it over Al Judge so that all you could see was that little bit of cane sticking out. Then he helped them steer the fat woman to the bed, and she sat down there, and the big skinny guy shoved her head down and began slapping her back. All this time she was laughing and crying and rocking around so they could hardly hold her.

If there was only some way of getting the light out, I could have dived out through the door and taken my chances. But the light switch was next to the door where I could see it but I couldn't reach it. All I could do was stay there on my knees and hope they would get out and leave me alone a minute. That was all I wanted, just one minute.

The fat woman was quieting down now, just saying, "Ahhh, ahhh," and the guy with the pants on stood watching and rubbing his hands as if they were freezing and he couldn't warm them up. Then he said, "I'll go out and fetch the police, Phelan," and Mr. Phelan, the big skinny one, said, very sore, "All right. All right. Get along with it," and the other one ran out of the room.

The fat woman started feeling better. She sat up and

kept pushing the others away and saying, "It's all right. Let me be. Let me be."

The little woman said, "It wasn't your fault you were taken like that, Mrs. Phelan. It was a terrible thing to see."

Mrs. Phelan kept rocking her body around. "It wasn't the dead, Mrs. Shane. I swear it wasn't the dead at all. It was the way this one could have been laying up in that hall now with a bullet through his head. That's all I was thinking of. I said to him, 'Anybody rings the bell this hour of the night is up to no good. Stay out of that hall,' and because God was good, he's alive to hear me say it again."

Mr. Phelan sat down on the bed and pulled a little piece of cigar out of his bathrobe pocket and started to chew on it. "Do you know what this means? A week's, maybe two weeks' rent before the police get it straightened out. And the room promised for tomorrow night."

Mrs. Phelan rocked worse than before. "There's a curse on this room. It's the devil's room. First the girl and now her brother all in a week. If it wasn't for these hard times, we'd never be able to rent it again sure."

Mrs. Shane said, "Her brother! I thought this was the new one who took the room," and Mrs. Phelan said, "No, Mrs. Shane, it's the brother himself. And a big man in the newspaper business. You'll see this all over the papers tomorrow."

"Will I, now!"

Mrs. Phelan said, "Still he went easier than she did. I could have told her. The day she took up with that cheap bartender, she put a curse on herself."

They were talking about my father. I knew that, and the blood was banging away so hard in my ears I was afraid I would miss something. I stopped looking through the crack and put my ear there, so I could hear better.

Mrs. Shane said, "Holy Mother Mary. And what was the story there?" and Mrs. Phelan said, "And what is the story any time? He got her into trouble sure enough, and then ran off and left her. It was no appendicitis attack she died from, Mrs. Shane. It was an A.B. and may the butcher who did it burn in hell forever for his sins!"

Mrs. Shane said, "Holy Mother Mary!" and Mr. Phelan said, "Agh. You're talking too much altogether."

"Am I? And where's the secret if the one it's promised to is laying cold and dead in front of you?"

That was what Al Judge was trying to tell me. My father got Frances in trouble, and that's why he was beaten up. And Frances died on account of it, so he had it coming to him. My father had it coming to him, and he never let me know. Now it was too late. The cops were coming and they would send me to the electric chair and it was all my father's fault for not telling me.

I started to cry. I was so scared on my knees in the dark there I couldn't help it. All I wanted was to get Al Judge back again so I could tell him everything was all right, but it was too late for that. Then I was afraid they would hear me crying, so I grabbed a dress and shoved it against my face. It had a little smell of perfume on it like Frances, and that made it worse.

Then I heard walking around and Mr. Phelan saying, "It's all right, Mrs. Shane. I can get her up myself," and then low talking in the hall and everything was real quiet.

I looked out through the crack and nobody was in the room. It was worse waiting in that closet that anything, and I had to take a chance. I went across the room as careful as I could and opened the door enough to see into the hall. I could hear Mr. and Mrs. Phelan still talking at the top of the stairs, but the hall was empty. In one second I was out of the front door and in the street.

Eighth Avenue was only a couple of steps away but I didn't go that way. There was too much light on it and I didn't want to go back to the bar anyhow. My father would be there waiting, and I wouldn't know what to tell him. Everything I did was wrong, and he might want to kill me for it, or turn me over to the cops right away. Down the street to Seventh Avenue it was darker, and I started running that way, with my legs shaking and my heart pounding so I couldn't take in enough air.

The wind was all gone, and in front of me across town the sky was beginning to get gray. It wasn't light yet, but I could tell it was getting near daytime and I was afraid of that too. In the nighttime, if you take care, you can get around without anybody seeing who you are, and it seems like people are more friendly and take it easier in the nighttime too.

By the time I ran to the corner, I had a stitch in my side so I had to stop and rest. My head was splitting too. It felt like a strap was pulling tighter and tighter around it, and my mouth was so dry I couldn't get up any saliva to swallow. I had to have some place where I could stop and think things over and figure them out. And I needed somebody to talk to who could maybe straighten me out.

Everything looked so easy when I started out, but I could see now I should never have got mixed up in this kind of older people's business. Because that's how it is with them. It doesn't look so bad on the outside, but when you start digging into it, it's worse trouble than you ever figured.

I needed somebody old to talk to and the only one I

could think of was Dr. Cooper. He was always talking about taking chances and that's what I did, so maybe he would understand. And Marion liked me plenty, so maybe she would understand too. If I went back there, I could sound them out and tell how they would take it, and if it looked all right I could open up.

And more than anything else right then, I needed a drink of water. I couldn't even think straight I was so thirsty, but if I drank and drank until I was filled up maybe it would be easier.

I went down three steps of the subway, and I stopped. All I had was the five-dollar bill, and I couldn't take any chances on making trouble with it. It was no good taking a taxi either. The driver would look at me and know around where I was going and that was the worst thing that could happen. I started walking down Seventh Avenue as fast as I could, which wasn't very fast.

All the time I was walking it kept getting lighter and lighter. There were trucks out now and more people on the street. If I walked too fast they turned around and looked at me, and any one of them might be a plain-clothes cop who knew about Peckinpaugh or even Al Judge and would grab me. So it was just as well I had to walk slow. Anyhow, when I tried to speed it up, the stitch in my side almost killed me.

Near Fourteenth Street there was a clock in a cigar-store window said almost six o'clock. There were a lot of people coming along now, mostly guys in old clothes with lunch boxes in their hands. I was surprised to see how many people went to work so early. There were cops too, walking along and shaking door handles on every store, and when I saw them coming I would stop and make believe to look in a store window until they went by.

When you see a place in the daytime, it's hard to find again at night, and it must work the other way too, because that's what threw me off. I found Barrow Street all right, but it was all daytime by then, and just when I got near there the street lights started to go out down the avenue. I turned down the block, but I couldn't figure exactly what house it was. There was the busted street light across the street, but the houses looked all the same.

I got good and scared. I started right near the alley where I saw the rats come out, and I went up into each house and looked at mailboxes. It took four houses before I found the one I wanted. Just a little hunk of paper and on it was Rostina-Gordon. I put my thumb on the bell underneath it and kept pushing as hard as I could.

The door started to go click-click-click, and I had to rattle it to catch it at the right time. Inside, when I looked up at all those stairs, I felt all in. I had to sit down and rest no matter what happened, and while I was doing it, I could hear Marion saying, "Right up here. Right up here," all the way on top.

It was no good resting. It didn't make me feel any better. I started going up the stairs, hanging on to the banister, and all that time she kept saying, "Right up here," so that I wanted to tell her it was all right, it was only me, but I didn't have the strength.

When I got to the top she was waiting there, and she looked the same as when I left her. Smeared lips and everything. Only when she saw the way I was coming up, she got all worried and grabbed my arm and almost pulled me into the house.

I just stood there looking at her, and she started shaking my sore arm good and hard so it hurt all over again. She kept shaking it and saying, "What is it? What's the matter?" and when I told her, it came out all different from the way I wanted it to.

It must have been so much on my mind I couldn't help it. That's what it must have been, because when she stopped shaking me, all I could say was, "I killed Al Judge, and I want a drink of water."

CHAPTER SIXTEEN

It's funny how people take things so differently. You go in and tell Mrs. Ehrlich there's nothing wrong, only little Gertrude is crying in the carriage outside, and the way she carries on and comes running out, you'd think something real bad had happened. Marion was upset, I could see that all right, but she didn't carry on any. First she pushed me down into the armchair, then she went into the kitchen and came running back with a glass of water and watched me while I drank it all down.

She stood in front of me with her eyes very shiny. Then she started looking all around the room, and flopping her hands up and down as if she had just washed them and was shaking the water off. "I should tell Lloyd, shouldn't I? But it's so early. He hates to be bothered so early."

I said, "You have to tell him. Tell him it's important. You have to!"

She was flopping her hands around and breathing so hard I could hear it. "He'll be so angry, George. Can't you wait a little while? You don't know what a temper he has."

The way she said that made everything seem crazy. Here I told her I killed somebody, and all she worried about was waking up Dr. Cooper. And I had to talk to him now. Talking to her only made things more tangled up. My hand hurt bad, and my head was splitting so everything was a little blurred, and I didn't know what to do.

I yelled, "Wake him up, will you! I have to talk to him! Why don't you wake him up?" and then the bedroom door came swinging open with a bang, and Dr. Cooper walked out into the room. His face was pasty white, as bad as Marion's, and his eyes were almost gummed together. All he had on was a pair of pajama pants, and he had white skin like a girl only with curly red hair all over his chest. He said, "Jesus! Why don't you two hire yourselves a hall?"

Tanya came out too, in a bathrobe and with her hair up in two little pigtails. She said, "Oh, all right, Lloyd. It's almost seven anyhow."

He said, "What do you mean, all right? Can't I ever

get any sleep around here? I'll be dead all day if I don't get any sleep." Then he said to Marion, "Why don't you fix your face. You look terrible," and she started to rub her hand around her mouth, scared like.

Tanya said, "All right, cut it out. What are you doing, George? Going now?" and Marion stopped rubbing her face and said, "He just came back. He killed somebody."

Dr. Cooper looked at her. "Sure he did. On his own milk-white charger. I know because I heard it galloping around the room all night."

He went over to the little table, very sore, and got a cigarette. Then he started looking around for a match but Tanya said, "Very funny, Lloyd. Now if you're so worried about your sleep, why don't you go back to bed?" and he threw the cigarette down and started walking back to the bedroom.

I didn't want that. I could see it wouldn't be easy to talk to him the way he felt, but I had to. I ran after him and got hold of his arm. "It's not a lie. It's true! I killed Al Judge, only I'm sorry now, and I don't know what to do! Don't you understand? I don't know what to do, and you've got to help me!"

He pulled away from me. Then he turned around and I could see he looked scared. "What do you mean, killed him? What did you do? Beat him up so bad you think he's dead?"

"I shot him!"

"Shot him? For Christ sake, you're drunk."

"I'm not drunk!" I pulled the gun from my pocket and held it out to show him. "I shot him with this."

Marion let out a squawk and went back so fast she hit the bed and sat down, but Tanya and Dr. Cooper just stood there looking at me, then the gun, and then me again.

Dr. Cooper said, "What are you making this up for? What's it all about?"

"I'm not making it up! Al Judge beat up my father with his cane and I killed him. I thought it was all right but then I found out something, and it isn't."

"Then what was all that about him firing you and you just wanted to get even?"

"I didn't say that. You said it, and I let you think it was so."

It looked like if he could have grabbed the gun he would have killed me right there. "I said it? Don't you go putting words into my mouth! What are you trying to do anyhow? Make me your alibi?"

"You don't understand! I don't want to get you in trouble. I don't know what to do. I want you to tell me what to do."

He shoved me back so hard I almost fell down. "First put that gun away! What do you want to do? Kill somebody else?"

I put the gun away in my pocket, and he started to rub his hand over his hair like a wild man. "You mean all that stuff about working for Judge was crap?"

"I don't work. I go to school. I'm too young to work!"

"Too young!"

"I never worked for Al Judge! I'm sixteen! I was only sixteen yesterday!"

I was looking at Dr. Cooper so hard I never even thought about Marion. It made my heart almost stop the way she jumped up and yelled, "You're not! You're not! Don't say a thing like that!"

Dr. Cooper didn't even look at her. He was looking at me with his mouth open, and I yelled, "That's how I had the tickets last night. It was my birthday present because I was sixteen!"

I think Marion must have gone crazy. She ran at Tanya and tried to rake her fingernails down Tanya's face, and all the time she was screaming, "You thought it was funny, didn't you? That's why you did it! You thought it was funny, didn't you?" until Tanya got hold of her and yelled back, "Stop that, Marion! I didn't know! I tell you I didn't know!"

Then all of a sudden Marion pulled herself loose and ran into the bedroom and slammed the door behind her. Tanya started to go to the door, but Dr. Cooper said, "Let her alone! She's better off in there."

She said, "I have to get you a robe anyhow. It's cold in here," and he said, "No. I want to get this straightened out first," so she just stood looking at me. She had a big scratch all down her cheek too, but it didn't seem to bother her.

Dr. Cooper said, "Why did Judge beat up your father?"

"Because my father got his sister in trouble. But I didn't know he did."

"You mean Judge's kid sister, Frances?"

"Yes. But I didn't know. I didn't even know she was his sister! How could I know if they don't have the same name even!"

"What same name? Why don't you try to make sense?"

"Her name is Frances Sedziaski. How could I know she was his sister?"

"For Christ sake, you didn't know that was his name too? It even means "judge" in Polish. He only started calling himself Judge when he took over the column!"

"I didn't know that! How could I know if nobody told me!"

"You didn't know anything at all, but you went out and killed him?"

He wasn't getting the idea at all. He just wasn't getting it. I said, "I saw the way he beat up my father and

I had to kill him. Because I didn't know what my father did."

"How did Judge find out what your father did? What was it anyhow? Rape?"

"No! Frances was in love with my father! She was crazy about him!"

"Well, for Christ sake, what happened? Did she tell Judge? Did he catch them together?"

I didn't know how to answer that. "Maybe he found out when Frances died."

"Died!"

"She died from an A.B. That was when he must have found out. When she died from the A.B."

Tanya said, "That's awful. Oh, that's awful," but Dr. Cooper didn't even listen to her. He said, "Where did you find all this out?" like he didn't believe me.

I said, "I was in a closet. After I killed him, I was in a closet and I heard people talking!"

He came close to me with his lips pulled back like a dog getting ready to fight. "That's a lot of bull, isn't it? But you think if you get me involved, I'll fix up your story for you. Is that what you're looking for?"

"It isn't bull! Honest to God, it isn't!"

"Then what did you come here for? You kill a man and then come running back to me! What do you want to get me mixed up in this for?"

He grabbed my overcoat and twisted it so tight that it cut into my chest and I was afraid to pull away. I said, "Honest to God, I don't want to get you in trouble. I don't want to get you in trouble, Dr. Cooper," but he kept pushing me to the front door and he wouldn't listen, and Tanya only stood there with that big scratch down her face and looked at me.

He said, "I'm telling you this, and, God damn it, get it into your head. You don't know me. You don't know me and you never saw me before in your life!"

The way he had me pushed up against the door I could hardly move, but I wouldn't let him get his hand on the doorknob. I yelled, "You've got to let me stay here! You can't chase me away! You've got to let me stay here!"

"I'm giving you the biggest break of your life by not turning you over to the cops right now! Open that door, and start going."

"You've got to let me stay here!"

"If you drag my name into this I'll kill you myself. Do you understand? I've got a wife upstate, and I don't want to do any explaining to her. And a job I'd be fired from tomorrow if this came out. Do you understand that?"

Tanya was standing in the middle of the room, and she wasn't looking at me any more. She was looking at

Dr. Cooper and you could see from the way she was breathing that she was mad. She said, "Is that what's bothering you? Go on, Lloyd, tell me. Is that what's on your mind? That pretty little wife with the big eyes, and that wonderful job you're so happy about?"

He let go of me all of a sudden and turned around to her. "Do you think I'm wrong if I don't want ten years of my life blown up by a crazy kid?"

She said, "No. No, but you want to watch yourself when you're drinking, Lloyd. That publicity job Olsen has waiting, that divorce, they all came out of the brandy bottle. Didn't they, Lloyd?"

"For Christ sake, Tanya! This isn't the time to start that!"

"You were lying all along, weren't you?"

"No, I wasn't. I meant everything I said. But it takes time. You just don't rush into things like that!"

"You're a riot, Lloyd. I don't rush into things like that. I'll be dead and gone before they happen."

He went over and tried to get hold of her, but she pushed him away. He said, "For Christ sake, Tanya!"

"Get away from me!" she yelled. "Get out of here!"

"Tanya!"

"Get your clothes and get out of here! And stay away from me!" She pointed at me. "And you get out of here too before I call the cops!"

Dr. Cooper was still trying to get hold of her, and he was yelling, "Don't you understand? I'm set! I can't take a chance!" and then Tanya hit him as hard as she could right across the face.

"Get out of here! Both of you! Get out of here!"

Even on the other side of the door after I got it closed again, I could hear her yelling that.

CHAPTER SEVENTEEN

I WAS afraid to go outside. I got as far as the little hall where the mailboxes were, and I waited there. There was a thin curtain over the front door, like a mosquito net, and I could look through it without anybody seeing me. Three or four times the street looked empty and I started to open the door, but then somebody would come along and I shut it quick.

I thought if only Al Judge would come alive again everything would be all right. Jesus Christ made a dead man come alive once, and if He would do that for me, I would never do anything wrong again. I would never even think anything wrong. I would be like a saint. I would only do good things, and if they wanted to burn me in a fire or cut me up on account of it, that would be all right.

The curtain smelled all dusty and old when I had my face against it, but I was crying and it felt better that way. I had it all straight in my mind. I would go into the first church I came to and tell the priest everything that happened. I wouldn't go to St Theresa, because they knew me there, but any other church was just as good. I would tell everything that happened and then the priest would give me penance and tell me what to do and I could start being good again. It made me feel better just thinking about it.

The next time the street looked empty I went outside and started walking along fast. I had my collar up and my head held down so nobody would get a good look at me. It was cold and gray out and other people were walking around the same way, but I was still scared. When somebody came walking along alone it wasn't so bad, but when a couple of people came along talking together I hated it. I thought they must be talking about me sure and then they would try to grab me, so I walked even faster.

I passed a lot of churches but they were all the wrong kind, and I was almost out of Greenwich Village before I came to the right one. I went up the stairs slow so I could get everything straight in my head before I started telling it to the priest, and then I pushed open the big door and went in.

They were having a Mass. It was after seven o'clock so of course it was seven-o'clock Mass. I had forgotten all about that. All the time I thought about going into the church I only saw the way it would be dark and quiet and nobody around. But there was a lot of people. And in a back row, right next to the aisle, there was a cop kneeling in his blue overcoat with the brass buttons in back of it, so if I took one step he might turn around and see me.

I was just inside the door. I reached around behind me with my hand and started pushing it open again. When it was open enough, I went through it fast, and down the stairs, only my legs were so weak they gave out near the bottom, and I fell on my hands and knees right out in the street.

I felt the gun slipping loose and I pushed it back hard into my pocket. My hat was near the gutter and a guy came running over with it. I was only afraid he would see my face good, so I grabbed the hat and put it on while I was running down the block. Maybe he was okay, but I couldn't take any chances. I kept changing around, running and walking, until I hit Fourteenth Street. Then I turned down toward Ninth Avenue and slowed up a little.

There was only one place left I could go. I had to get back to the bar without anybody seeing me and take a chance my father would listen to me. I couldn't figure what he would say or do, but whatever it was it would be better than going crazy walking around and around the streets.

There were some stores open on Ninth Avenue already, and when I same to them I went by as fast as I could, and then I slowed down by the ones that weren't open yet. That's how it happened I was leaning up against the door of Mr. Triola's barbershop when I looked down the block and saw the cops coming out of the bar. All I could do was flatten myself up against the door and pray none of the cops would look down the block my way.

There were three cops in uniform and another guy, and they walked to a big black sedan that was parked there. They stood next to it, and the guy talked to them and pointed with his hand, and I saw it was Peckinpaugh. It sent a chill through me, and I pressed so hard against the door my shoulders hurt.

But he didn't see me. He kept talking, and the other cops kept shaking their heads yes, and then he and two of the cops got into the car and drove right past me, very fast and with a lot of noise.

The cop that was left stood looking after them a little while, banging his night stick into his other hand like he was sore, and I saw it was Kennealy. Then he turned and walked back into Mr. Ehrlich's store. I could hear the door slam after him.

I couldn't take a chance on passing in front of the candy store now. I ran across the street and down the block on that side until I came opposite the bar. I stopped to see if everything was still quiet around Mr. Ehrlich's, and then I ran back across the street to the bar. If the door was locked I was ready to kick it in, but it was all right. Just the way I left it. I went in quick and then pushed the door shut so it wouldn't make any noise.

It was empty inside. If I had come five minutes before, I would have run into all those cops, but now it was empty and quiet the same as when I left it. The big puddle of whisky was only a dark spot on the floor now, and my busted glasses were in the middle of it. My plate was still on the table and the coke bottle half-full. I grabbed it and drank it all down the way it was. It was lukewarm and flat, but it tasted wonderful.

I didn't want to go upstairs but I had to. I figured I would be the first one to tell my father about what happened, but I knew the cops must have done that. And maybe they told him a lot of lies. I had to go up and straighten him out if he would only listen to me.

I went through the back door into the hall. The yard didn't look exciting any more. It looked cold and gray, and Mr. Ehrlich's peach tree was standing there like a dead thing. Then something pushed me and I froze up, all sick inside, until I looked down and saw it was Flanagan's cat. That was when I heard the talking upstairs.

It wasn't loud enough to hear the words. I went up the first two steps, but I still couldn't hear them, and I had to. I started going up the rest of the way, flattened against the wall, and looking around to make sure nobody was watching me. There were two people talking in the parlor, and one of them was my father.

He said, "Don't, Mr. Judge! I tell you I don't know. You saw them go over the place. I tell you I don't know!" and Al Judge said, "I warned you, LaMain. I'll tear you apart if you don't start talking! Where is he?"

I felt like I was walking in my sleep. I was standing in front of the door, looking at Al Judge's face all blood-red, and watching him slap the cane into his other hand like Kennealy was doing with the night stick, and listening to his voice come from between his teeth. There was bandage and tape all along the side of his head, there wasn't any white scarf, but it was him all right. It was a miracle.

My father was trying to move back, but he was up against the big armchair and he couldn't. He said, "Don't, Mr. Judge! I swear I don't know!" and Al Judge yelled, "God damn you, LaMain! I warned you!"

And then the cane was up in the air. Up over his head the same way I remembered it, only it wasn't meant for me. It was meant for my father, and it would come down across the stripes on his back and he would scream and fall down and the whole thing would start all over again.

The gun was in my hand. I didn't think about pulling it out or anything because it was in my hand. I only thought, the best way to hold it is with both hands because it kicks back so hard, and I held it tight with both hands and squeezed it *crash*, squeezed it *crash*, again and again, until it went click-click-click, and Al Judge grabbed his belly with both hands and fell over on his face, and the cane was lying in the armchair.

I didn't know Flanagan was there all that time. He grabbed me by one arm, and my father got me by the other and pulled the gun out of my hand. He held it out, showing it to me and yelling something, but my ears were ringing and I couldn't hear him. I thought I was going to pass out right in the door, but Flanagan got an arm around me and tried to steer me to a chair there.

Then I heard what my father was saying. He was yelling, with his face all twisted like a crazy man, "It's her blood! Do you hear? It's her blood, and you'll end the same way!"

He didn't know Kennealy had come up. None of us knew it. He was standing at the top of the stairs with his gun pointed at my father, and he was bent over like a football player getting ready to tackle somebody.

He yelled, "LaMain! Drop it!" and there was my father twisting around surprised with the gun still in his hand, and Kennealy yelled, "LaMain!" and his gun went off, and my father kept twisting all the way around until he hit the little table with the radio and the picture on it. It went over, and he went over with it, and he lay there quiet.

That was all. Only Flanagan kneeling over him with his overcoat on and his torn old sweater showing. He was kneeling there, and I think he was crying, and he was pushing his teeth in with the back of his hand and saying over and over, "Ah, Kennealy, the gun was empty. Didn't you know, Kennealy? The gun was empty."

Over and over.

CHAPTER EIGHTEEN

IT WAS quiet in the bedroom. Quiet and dark. Sitting on the edge of the bed with Flanagan next to me, and looking at the big double doors, it felt like the parlor and everything in it was a thousand miles away. You could hear the cops and the guys from the newspapers walking around and talking, but as long as the doors were closed I didn't care.

It was different when they had me in the parlor. They asked me questions so fast I couldn't think, and I had to put my hands over my ears and yell, "Shut up! Shut up!" until they stopped. Then Flanagan and Kennealy started talking to an old guy who was there, and he let Flanagan take me into the bedroom.

It was good talking to Flanagan in the dark. It was almost like talking to myself, and it helped me put things together. When we sat on the bed, he whispered, "Keep your head screwed on. They think your father killed the man, do you see? And to my way of thinking, it's enough he died for it. Now, for God sake, tell me everything so we'll know what kind of a story to give them."

So I told him. I told him everything from the time Al Judge came into the bar all the way to the end. Sometimes I couldn't remember exactly what happened or somebody's name, but it was so important to me that I should, that I stopped and figured it out until I had it right. And all the time I didn't feel like I was doing the talking at all. It felt like the words were coming out by themselves and all I had to do was steer them along.

When I was done, Flanagan sat quiet a little, and then he said, "Peckinpaugh is the man to be afraid of, all right. He'll twist and turn everything you've done until he has you where he wants you."

I said, "What will he do to me?"

"It may be, mind you I don't say for sure, but it may be he'll try to put the killing on you. He's the one to keep in mind while we fix up the story."

I said, "Why didn't you stop me? I wouldn't have done it, only nobody stopped me!"

"Shh! Have you got stones in the head? When you

weren't home after twelve, your father had me walking the streets all night in the blackness looking for you. Only when Judge came with the cops did we have an idea what happened and your poor father near went out of his mind."

I said, "I don't care! It was his fault! Why didn't he tell me about Frances? I wouldn't have done it if I knew all about what happened!"

Flanagan said, "Quiet! Who's to pin the fault on anyone? He never told the girl he would marry her, but she said no matter. When she came crying, and said she was in trouble and he would have to marry her Johnny-on-the-spot, what could he do? He gave her the only advice he could.

"Was it his fault if she died in her room from poisoning after the operation? Up to the end she hardly spoke a word about her brother, the way she hated him for his bullying ways, but the priest got him there before she went, and that's how it all came out. It was nobody's fault, the way it happened."

"It was! Why didn't he marry her? He liked her all right, didn't he? Then why didn't he marry her?"

"Marry her? Christ Jesus and the angels! How could he marry anyone when he's still married to your mother?"

"But she's dead! My mother is dead!"

He started rocking from side to side so his shoulder kept hitting me. "Ah, Jesus, it's out now and what's the difference with him laying in there. He could have been free of your mother any day he said the word, but he would never say it. He could never have her, but the way he was mad about her, he would never cut the ties between them.

"That was what he carried around inside of him, night and day. All he ever feared in his life was you would find out, and it would hurt you like it hurt him. He had you on one side and her on the other, and he was torn between you night and day."

I whispered, "But she's dead. He told me himself she was dead long ago."

"She's in prison for life. She'll live there, and she'll die there, but as long as your father had breath in his body, she was the only woman for him. And she was no good. Smart and beautiful, and no good at all."

"But what did she do?"

"What did she do? She had you squalling in a baby bed upstairs, and your father working his head off to make money for her, and all that time she was carrying on with another man! The bar was on the other side of town then, and from the day I went to work there, I could see she was no good. All that time carrying on with another man until the day he threw her over for someone else's wife, and she found him out and shot his in his bed. And even knowing the truth, your father would have given his life to save her from what she had coming."

"He never told me that. He never told me anything about it."

"Everything he did from then on was to save you from knowing. If I ever told you this when he was alive, he would have had my life."

My eyes were getting so used to the dark now, I could almost see myself in the mirror, and I saw I still had the black hat on. I took it off and started wiping it around so it would be the way my father liked it. Then I couldn't help it. I crumpled it up and squeezed it as tight as I could in my hands and held it that way, and it felt good.

Flanagan said, "That's how it is with some men. There's only one woman in the world for them, and if it's the wrong one, no matter. They call their curse a blessing and carry it inside of them to the grave. That was your father."

I said, "He was all right."

Flanagan said, "He wouldn't want you to end up the same as she did. Let me tell you what to say now."

"No. He was all right."

"Then listen now."

I said, "No. You don't understand. You just don't understand."

"Have you gone crazy? You'll do the way I say!"

Somebody knocked on the double doors and said, "Hey, you guys," and Flanagan jumped up and said, "Right away! He'll be feeling better right away!"

Then he got me by the shoulders and started shaking me so my head rocked. "Listen to me!" he said into my ear. "Listen to me!"

I said, "No. I want to tell them what happened."

"What are you saying?"

I had the hat squeezed tight in my hands. I said, "I want to tell them what really happened."

"Oh, Jesus, you're crazy! Do you hear? You're crazy for sure!"

But I wasn't. It was only that I saw everything straight now, and how my father took that beating from Al Judge because, the way he looked at it, it was coming to him. All his life, he took what was coming to him and never said anything about it because he was that kind of a guy.

Flanagan didn't understand. He just didn't understand that even if my father was dead, it was the most important thing in the world that people mustn't think he was a bad guy. Because he wasn't.

He wasn't like that at all.

He was all right.

DISCUSSION QUESTIONS

- Was George's character a sympathetic one? Do you think he made the right choice in the end?
- The narrative structure of one long night recurs throughout literary history. How does Ellin's version compare to others you may have read?
- Did any aspects of the plot date the story? If so, which?
- Would the story be different if it were set in the present day? If so, how?
- Did the social context of the time play a role in the narrative? If so, how?
- Did this book remind you of any present day authors? If so, which?

OTTO PENZLER PRESENTS
AMERICAN MYSTERY CLASSICS

All titles are available in hardcover and in trade paperback.

Order from your favorite bookstore or from
The Mysterious Bookshop, 58 Warren Street, New York, N.Y. 10007
(www.mysteriousbookshop.com).

Charlotte Armstrong, ***The Chocolate Cobweb.*** When Amanda Garth was born, a mix-up caused the hospital to briefly hand her over to the prestigious Garrison family instead of to her birth parents. The error was quickly fixed, Amanda was never told, and the secret was forgotten for twenty-three years … until her aunt revealed it in casual conversation. But what if the initial switch never actually occurred? **Introduction by A. J. Finn.**

Charlotte Armstrong, ***The Unsuspected.*** First published in 1946, this suspenseful novel opens with a young woman who has ostensibly hanged herself, leaving a suicide note. Her friend doesn't believe it and begins an investigation that puts her own life in jeopardy. It was filmed in 1947 by Warner Brothers, starring Claude Rains and Joan Caulfield. **Introduction by Otto Penzler.**

Anthony Boucher, ***The Case of the Baker Street Irregulars.*** When a studio announces a new hard-boiled Sherlock Holmes film, the Baker Street Irregulars begin a campaign to discredit it. Attempting to mollify them, the producers invite members to the set, where threats are received, each referring to one of the original Holmes tales, followed by murder. Fortunately, the amateur sleuths use Holmesian lessons to solve the crime. **Introduction by Otto Penzler.**

Anthony Boucher, ***Rocket to the Morgue.*** Hilary Foulkes has made so many enemies that it is difficult to speculate who was responsible for stabbing him nearly to death in a room with only one door through which no one was seen entering or leaving. This classic locked room mystery is populated by such thinly disguised science fiction legends as Robert Heinlein, L. Ron Hubbard, and John W. Campbell. **Introduction by F. Paul Wilson.**

Fredric Brown, ***The Fabulous Clipjoint.*** Brown's outstanding mystery won an Edgar as the best first novel of the year (1947). When Wallace Hunter is found dead in an alley after a long night of drinking, the police don't really care. But his teenage son Ed and his uncle Am, the carnival worker, are convinced that some things don't add up and the crime isn't what it seems to be. **Introduction by Lawrence Block.**

John Dickson Carr, ***The Crooked Hinge.*** Selected by a group of mystery experts as one of the 15 best impossible crime novels ever written, this is one of Gideon Fell's greatest challenges. Estranged from his family for 25 years, Sir John Farnleigh returns to England from America to claim his inheritance but another person turns up claiming that he can prove he is the real Sir John. Inevitably, one of them is murdered. **Introduction by Charles Todd.**

John Dickson Carr, ***The Eight of Swords.*** When Gideon Fell arrives at a crime scene, it appears to be straightforward enough. A man has been shot to death in an unlocked room and the likely perpetrator was a recent visitor. But Fell discovers inconsistencies and his investigations are complicated by an apparent poltergeist, some American gangsters, and two meddling amateur sleuths. **Introduction by Otto Penzler.**

John Dickson Carr, ***The Mad Hatter Mystery.*** A prankster has been stealing top hats all around London. Gideon Fell suspects that the same person may be responsible for the theft of a manuscript of a long-lost story by Edgar Allan Poe. The hats reappear in unexpected but conspicuous places but, when one is found on the head of a corpse by the Tower of London, it is evident that the thefts are more than pranks. **Introduction by Otto Penzler.**

John Dickson Carr, ***The Plague Court Murders.*** When murder occurs in a locked hut on Plague Court, an estate haunted by the ghost of a hangman's assistant who died a victim of the black death, Sir Henry Merrivale seeks a logical solution to a ghostly crime. A spiritual medium employed to rid the house of his spirit is found stabbed to death in a locked stone hut on the grounds, surrounded by an untouched circle of mud. **Introduction by Michael Dirda.**

John Dickson Carr, ***The Red Widow Murders.*** In a "haunted" mansion, the room known as the Red Widow's Chamber proves lethal to all who spend the night. Eight people investigate and the one who draws the ace of spades must sleep in it. The room is locked from the inside and watched all night by the others. When the door is unlocked, the victim has been poisoned. Enter Sir Henry Merrivale to solve the crime. **Introduction by Tom Mead.**

Frances Crane, ***The Turquoise Shop.*** In an arty little New Mexico town, Mona Brandon has arrived from the East and becomes the subject of gossip about her money, her influence, and the corpse in the nearby desert who may be her husband. Pat Holly, who runs the local gift shop, is as interested as anyone in the goings on—but even more in Pat Abbott, the detective investigating the possible murder. **Introduction by Anne Hillerman.**

Todd Downing, ***Vultures in the Sky.*** There is no end to the series of terrifying events that befall a luxury train bound for Mexico. First, a man dies when the train passes through a dark tunnel, then it comes to an abrupt stop in the middle of the desert. More deaths occur when night falls and the passengers panic when they realize they are trapped with a murderer on the loose. **Introduction by James Sallis.**

Mignon G. Eberhart, ***Murder by an Aristocrat.*** Nurse Keate is called to help a man who has been "accidentally" shot in the shoulder. When he is murdered while convalescing, it is clear that there was no accident. Although a killer is loose in the mansion, the family seems more concerned that news of the murder will leave their circle. *The New Yorker* wrote than "Eberhart can weave an almost flawless mystery." **Introduction by Nancy Pickard.**

Erle Stanley Gardner, ***The Case of the Baited Hook.*** Perry Mason gets a phone call in the middle of the night and his potential client says it's urgent, that he has two one-thousand-dollar bills that he will give him as a retainer, with an additional ten-thousand whenever he is called on to represent him. When Mason takes the case, it is not for the caller but for a beautiful woman whose identity is hidden behind a mask. **Introduction by Otto Penzler.**

Erle Stanley Gardner, ***The Case of the Borrowed Brunette.*** A mysterious man named Mr. Hines has advertised a job for a woman who has to fulfill very specific physical requirements. Eva Martell, pretty but struggling in her career as a model, takes the job but her aunt smells a rat and hires Perry Mason to investigate. Her fears are realized when Hines turns up in the apartment with a bullet hole in his head. **Introduction by Otto Penzler.**

Erle Stanley Gardner, ***The Case of the Careless Kitten.*** Helen Kendal receives a mysterious phone call from her vanished uncle Franklin, long presumed dead, who urges her to contact Perry Mason. Soon, she finds herself the main suspect in the murder of an unfamiliar man. Her kitten has just survived a poisoning attempt—as has her aunt Matilda. What is the connection between Franklin's return and the murder attempts? **Introduction by Otto Penzler.**

Erle Stanley Gardner, ***The Case of the Rolling Bones.*** One of Gardner's most successful Perry Mason novels opens with a clear case of blackmail, though the person being blackmailed claims he isn't. It is not long before the police are searching for someone wanted for killing the same man in two different states—thirty-three years apart. The confounding puzzle of what happened to the dead man's toes is a challenge. **Introduction by Otto Penzler.**

Erle Stanley Gardner, ***The Case of the Shoplifter's Shoe.*** Most cases for Perry Mason involve murder but here he is hired because a young woman fears her aunt is a kleptomaniac. Sarah may not have been precisely the best guardian for a collection of valuable diamonds and, sure enough, they go missing. When the jeweler is found shot dead, Sarah is spotted leaving the murder scene with a bundle of gems stuffed in her purse. **Introduction by Otto Penzler.**

Erle Stanley Gardner, ***The Bigger They Come.*** Gardner's first novel using the pseudonym A.A. Fair starts off a series featuring the large and loud Bertha Cool and her employee, the small and meek Donald Lam. Given the job of delivering divorce papers to an evident crook,

Lam can't find him—but neither can the police. The *Los Angeles Times* called this book: "Breathlessly dramatic … an original." **Introduction by Otto Penzler.**

Frances Noyes Hart, *The Bellamy Trial.* Inspired by the real-life Hall-Mills case, the most sensational trial of its day, this is the story of Stephen Bellamy and Susan Ives, accused of murdering Bellamy's wife Madeleine. Eight days of dynamic testimony, some true, some not, make headlines for an enthralled public. Rex Stout called this historic courtroom thriller one of the ten best mysteries of all time. **Introduction by Hank Phillippi Ryan.**

H.F. Heard, *A Taste for Honey.* The elderly Mr. Mycroft quietly keeps bees in Sussex, where he is approached by the reclusive and somewhat misanthropic Mr. Silchester, whose honey supplier was found dead, stung to death by her bees. Mycroft, who shares many traits with Sherlock Holmes, sets out to find the vicious killer. Rex Stout described it as "sinister … a tale well and truly told." **Introduction by Otto Penzler.**

Dolores Hitchens, *The Alarm of the Black Cat.* Detective fiction aficionado Rachel Murdock has a peculiar meeting with a little girl and a dead toad, sparking her curiosity about a love triangle that has sparked anger. When the girl's great grandmother is found dead, Rachel and her cat Samantha work with a friend in the Los Angeles Police Department to get to the bottom of things. **Introduction by David Handler.**

Dolores Hitchens, *The Cat Saw Murder.* Miss Rachel Murdock, the highly intelligent 70-year-old amateur sleuth, is not entirely heartbroken when her slovenly, unattractive, bridge-cheating niece is murdered. Miss Rachel is happy to help the socially maladroit and somewhat bumbling Detective Lieutenant Stephen Mayhew, retaining her composure when a second brutal murder occurs. **Introduction by Joyce Carol Oates.**

Dorothy B. Hughes, *Dread Journey.* A big-shot Hollywood producer has worked on his magnum opus for years, hiring and firing one beautiful starlet after another. But Kitten Agnew's contract won't allow her to be fired, so she fears she might be terminated more permanently. Together with the producer on a train journey from Hollywood to Chicago, Kitten becomes more terrified with each passing mile. **Introduction by Sarah Weinman.**

Dorothy B. Hughes, *Ride the Pink Horse.* When Sailor met Willis Douglass, he was just a poor kid who Douglass groomed to work as a confidential secretary. As the senator became increasingly corrupt, he knew he could count on Sailor to clean up his messes. No longer a senator, Douglass flees Chicago for Santa Fe, leaving behind a murder rap and Sailor as the prime suspect. Seeking vengeance, Sailor follows. **Introduction by Sara Paretsky.**

Dorothy B. Hughes, *The So Blue Marble.* Set in the glamorous world of New York high society, this novel became a suspense classic as twins from Europe try to steal a rare and beautiful gem owned by an aristocrat whose sister is an even more menacing presence. *The New Yorker* called it "Extraordinary … [Hughes'] brilliant descriptive powers make and unmake reality." **Introduction by Otto Penzler.**

W. Bolingbroke Johnson, *The Widening Stain.* After a cocktail party, the attractive Lucie Coindreau, a "black-eyed, black-haired Frenchwoman" visits the rare books wing of the library and apparently takes a head-first fall from an upper gallery. Dismissed as a horrible accident, it seems dubious when Professor Hyett is strangled while reading a priceless 12th-century manuscript, which has gone missing. **Introduction by Nicholas A. Basbanes**

Baynard Kendrick, *Blind Man's Bluff.* Blinded in World War II, Duncan Maclain forms a successful private detective agency, aided by his two dogs. Here, he is called on to solve the case of a blind man who plummets from the top of an eight-story building, apparently with no one present except his dead-drunk son. **Introduction by Otto Penzler.**

Baynard Kendrick, *The Odor of Violets.* Duncan Maclain, a blind former intelligence officer, is asked to investigate the murder of an actor in his Greenwich Village apartment. This would cause a stir at any time but, when the actor possesses secret government plans that then go missing, it's enough to interest the local police as well as the American government and Maclain, who suspects a German spy plot. **Introduction by Otto Penzler.**

C. Daly King, *Obelists at Sea.* On a cruise ship traveling from New York to Paris, the lights of the smoking room briefly go out, a gunshot crashes through the night, and a man is dead. Two detectives are on board but so are four psychiatrists who believe their professional knowledge can solve the case by understanding the psyche of the killer—each with a different theory. **Introduction by Martin Edwards.**

Jonathan Latimer, *Headed for a Hearse.* Featuring Bill Crane, the booze-soaked Chicago private detective, this humorous hard-boiled novel was filmed as *The Westland Case* in 1937 starring Preston Foster. Robert Westland has been framed for the grisly murder of his wife in a room with doors and windows locked from the inside. As the day of his execution nears, he relies on Crane to find the real murderer. **Introduction by Max Allan Collins**

Lange Lewis, ***The Birthday Murder.*** Victoria is a successful novelist and screenwriter and her husband is a movie director so their marriage seems almost too good to be true. Then, on her birthday, her happy new life comes crashing down when her husband is murdered using a method of poisoning that was described in one of her books. She quickly becomes the leading suspect. **Introduction by Randal S. Brandt.**

Frances and Richard Lockridge, ***Death on the Aisle.*** In one of the most beloved books to feature Mr. and Mrs. North, the body of a wealthy backer of a play is found dead in a seat of the 45th Street Theater. Pam is thrilled to engage in her favorite pastime—playing amateur sleuth—much to the annoyance of Jerry, her publisher husband. The Norths inspired a stage play, a film, and long-running radio and TV series. **Introduction by Otto Penzler.**

John P. Marquand, ***Your Turn, Mr. Moto.*** The first novel about Mr. Moto, originally titled *No Hero,* is the story of a World War I hero pilot who finds himself jobless during the Depression. In Tokyo for a big opportunity that falls apart, he meets a Japanese agent and his Russian colleague and the pilot suddenly finds himself caught in a web of intrigue. Peter Lorre played Mr. Moto in a series of popular films. **Introduction by Lawrence Block.**

Stuart Palmer, ***The Penguin Pool Murder.*** The first adventure of schoolteacher and dedicated amateur sleuth Hildegarde Withers occurs at the New York Aquarium when she and her young students notice a corpse in one of the tanks. It was published in 1931 and filmed the next year, starring Edna May Oliver as the American Miss Marple—though much funnier than her English counterpart. **Introduction by Otto Penzler.**

Stuart Palmer, ***The Puzzle of the Happy Hooligan.*** New York City schoolteacher Hildegarde Withers cannot resist "assisting" homicide detective Oliver Piper. In this novel, she is on vacation in Hollywood and on the set of a movie about Lizzie Borden when the screenwriter is found dead. Six comic films about Withers appeared in the 1930s, most successfully starring Edna May Oliver. **Introduction by Otto Penzler.**

Otto Penzler, ed., ***Golden Age Bibliomysteries.*** Stories of murder, theft, and suspense occur with alarming regularity in the unlikely world of books and bibliophiles, including bookshops, libraries, and private rare book collections, written by such giants of the mystery genre as Ellery Queen, Cornell Woolrich, Lawrence G. Blochman, Vincent Starrett, and Anthony Boucher. **Introduction by Otto Penzler.**

Otto Penzler, ed., ***Golden Age Detective Stories.*** The history of American mystery fiction has its pantheon of authors who have influenced and entertained readers for nearly a century, reaching its peak during the Golden Age, and this collection pays homage to the work of the most acclaimed: Cornell Woolrich, Erle Stanley Gardner, Craig Rice, Ellery Queen, Dorothy B. Hughes, Mary Roberts Rinehart, and more. **Introduction by Otto Penzler.**

Otto Penzler, ed., ***Golden Age Locked Room Mysteries.*** The so-called impossible crime category reached its zenith during the 1920s, 1930s, and 1940s, and this volume includes the greatest of the great authors who mastered the form: John Dickson Carr, Ellery Queen, C. Daly King, Clayton Rawson, and Erle Stanley Gardner. Like great magicians, these literary conjurors will baffle and delight readers. **Introduction by Otto Penzler.**

Ellery Queen, ***The Adventures of Ellery Queen.*** These stories are the earliest short works to feature Queen as a detective and are among the best of the author's fair-play mysteries. So many of the elements that comprise the gestalt of Queen may be found in these tales: alternate solutions, the dying clue, a bizarre crime, and the author's ability to find fresh variations of works by other authors. **Introduction by Otto Penzler.**

Ellery Queen, *The American Gun Mystery*. A rodeo comes to New York City at the Colosseum. The headliner is Buck Horne, the once popular film cowboy who opens the show leading a charge of forty whooping cowboys until they pull out their guns and fire into the air. Buck falls to the ground, shot dead. The police instantly lock the doors to search everyone but the offending weapon has completely vanished. **Introduction by Otto Penzler.**

Ellery Queen, *The Chinese Orange Mystery*. The offices of publisher Donald Kirk have seen strange events but nothing like this. A strange man is found dead with two long spears alongside his back. And, though no one was seen entering or leaving the room, everything has been turned backwards or upside down: pictures face the wall, the victim's clothes are worn backwards, the rug upside down. Why in the world? **Introduction by Otto Penzler.**

Ellery Queen, *The Dutch Shoe Mystery*. Millionaire philanthropist Abagail Doorn falls into a coma and she is rushed to the hospital she funds for an emergency operation by one of the leading surgeons on the East Coast. When she is wheeled into the operating theater, the sheet covering her body is pulled back to reveal her garroted corpse—the first of a series of murders **Introduction by Otto Penzler.**

Ellery Queen, *The Egyptian Cross Mystery*. A small-town schoolteacher is found dead, headed, and tied to a T-shaped cross on December 25th, inspiring such sensational headlines as "Crucifixion on Christmas Day." Amateur sleuth Ellery Queen is so intrigued he travels to Virginia but fails to solve the crime. Then a similar murder takes place on New York's Long Island—and then another. **Introduction by Otto Penzler.**

Ellery Queen, *The Siamese Twin Mystery*. When Ellery and his father encounter a raging forest fire on a mountain, their only hope is to drive up to an isolated hillside manor owned by a secretive surgeon and his strange guests. While playing solitaire in the middle of the night, the doctor is shot. The only clue is a torn playing card. Suspects include a society beauty, a valet, and conjoined twins. **Introduction by Otto Penzler.**

Ellery Queen, *The Spanish Cape Mystery*. Amateur detective Ellery Queen arrives in the resort town of Spanish Cape soon after a young woman and her uncle are abducted by a gun-toting, one-eyed giant. The next day, the woman's somewhat dicey boyfriend is found murdered—totally naked under a black fedora and opera cloak. **Introduction by Otto Penzler.**

Patrick Quentin, *A Puzzle for Fools*. Broadway producer Peter Duluth takes to the bottle when his wife dies but enters a sanitarium to dry out. Malevolent events plague the hospital, including when Peter hears his own voice intone, "There will be murder." And there is. He investigates, aided by a young woman who is also a patient. This is the first of nine mysteries featuring Peter and Iris Duluth. **Introduction by Otto Penzler.**

Clayton Rawson, *Death from a Top Hat*. When the New York City Police Department is baffled by an apparently impossible crime, they call on The Great Merlini, a retired stage magician who now runs a Times Square magic shop. In his first case, two occultists have been murdered in a room locked from the inside, their bodies positioned to form a pentagram. **Introduction by Otto Penzler.**

Craig Rice, *Eight Faces at Three*. Gin-soaked John J. Malone, defender of the guilty, is notorious for getting his culpable clients off. It's the innocent ones who are problems. Like Holly Inglehart, accused of piercing the black heart of her well-heeled aunt Alexandria with a lovely Florentine paper cutter. No one who knew the old battle-ax liked her, but Holly's prints were found on the murder weapon. **Introduction by Lisa Lutz.**

Craig Rice, *Home Sweet Homicide*. Known as the Dorothy Parker of mystery fiction for her memorable wit, Craig Rice was the first detective writer to appear on the cover of *Time* magazine. This comic mystery features two kids who are trying to find a husband for their widowed mother while she's engaged in sleuthing. Filmed with the same title in 1946 with Peggy Ann Garner and Randolph Scott. **Introduction by Otto Penzler.**

Mary Roberts Rinehart, *The Album*. Crescent Place is a quiet enclave of wealthy people in which nothing ever happens—until a bedridden old woman is attacked by an intruder with an ax. *The New York Times* stated: "All Mary Roberts Rinehart mystery stories are good, but this one is better." **Introduction by Otto Penzler.**

Mary Roberts Rinehart, *The Haunted Lady*. The arsenic in her sugar bowl was wealthy widow Eliza Fairbanks' first clue that somebody wanted her dead. Nightly visits of bats, birds, and rats, obviously aimed at scaring the dowager to death, was the second. Eliza calls the police, who send nurse Hilda Adams, the amateur sleuth they refer to as "Miss Pinkerton," to work undercover to discover the culprit. **Introduction by Otto Penzler.**

Mary Roberts Rinehart, *Miss Pinkerton*. Hilda Adams is a nurse, not a detective, but she is observant and smart and so it is common for Inspector Patton to call on her for help. Her success results in his calling her "Miss Pinkerton." *The New Republic* wrote: "From thousands of hearts and homes the cry will go up: Thank God for Mary Roberts Rinehart." **Introduction by Carolyn Hart.**

Mary Roberts Rinehart, *The Red Lamp*. Professor William Porter refuses to believe that the seaside manor he's just inherited is haunted but he has to convince his wife to move in. However, he soon sees evidence of the occult phenomena of which the townspeople speak. Whether it is a spirit or a human being, Porter accepts that there is a connection to the rash of murders that have terrorized the countryside. **Introduction by Otto Penzler.**

Mary Roberts Rinehart, *The Wall*. For two decades, Mary Roberts Rinehart was the second-best-selling author in America (only Sinclair Lewis outsold her) and was beloved for her tales of suspense. In a magnificent mansion, the ex-wife of one of the owners turns up making demands and is found dead the next day. And there are more dark secrets lying behind the walls of the estate. **Introduction by Otto Penzler.**

Joel Townsley Rogers, *The Red Right Hand*. This extraordinary whodunnit that is as puzzling as it is terrifying was identified by crime fiction scholar Jack Adrian as "one of the dozen or so finest mystery novels of the 20th century." A deranged killer sends a doctor on a quest for the truth—deep into the recesses of his own mind—when he and his bride-to-be elope but pick up a terrifying sharp-toothed hitch-hiker. **Introduction by Joe R. Lansdale.**

Roger Scarlett, *Cat's Paw*. The family of the wealthy old bachelor Martin Greenough cares far more about his money than they do about him. For his birthday, he invites all his potential heirs to his mansion to tell them what they hope to hear. Before he can disburse funds, however, he is murdered, and the Boston Police Department's big problem is that there are too many suspects. **Introduction by Curtis Evans**

Vincent Starrett, *Dead Man Inside*. 1930s Chicago is a tough town but some crimes are more bizarre than others. Customers arrive at a haberdasher to find a corpse in the window and a sign on the door: *Dead Man Inside! I am Dead. The store will not open today.* This is just one of a series of odd murders that terrorizes the city. Reluctant detective Walter Ghost leaps into action to learn what is behind the plague. **Introduction by Otto Penzler.**

Vincent Starrett, *The Great Hotel Murder*. Theater critic and amateur sleuth Riley Blackwood investigates a murder in a Chicago hotel where the dead man had changed rooms with a stranger who had registered under a fake name. *The New York Times* described it as "an ingenious plot with enough complications to keep the reader guessing." **Introduction by Lyndsay Faye.**

Vincent Starrett, *Murder on 'B' Deck*. Walter Ghost, a psychologist, scientist, explorer, and former intelligence officer, is on a cruise ship and his friend novelist Dunsten Mollock, a Nigel Bruce-like Watson whose role is to offer occasional comic relief, accommodates when he fails to leave the ship before it takes off. Although they make mistakes along the way, the amateur sleuths solve the shipboard murders. **Introduction by Ray Betzner.**

Phoebe Atwood Taylor, *The Cape Cod Mystery*. Vacationers have flocked to Cape Cod to avoid the heat wave that hit the Northeast and find their holiday unpleasant when the area is flooded with police trying to find the murderer of a muckraking journalist who took a cottage for the season. Finding a solution falls to Asey Mayo, "the Cape Cod Sherlock," known for his worldly wisdom, folksy humor, and common sense. **Introduction by Otto Penzler.**

S. S. Van Dine, ***The Benson Murder Case.*** The first of 12 novels to feature Philo Vance, the most popular and influential detective character of the early part of the 20th century. When wealthy stockbroker Alvin Benson is found shot to death in a locked room in his mansion, the police are baffled until the erudite flaneur and art collector arrives on the scene. Paramount filmed it in 1930 with William Powell as Vance. **Introduction by Ragnar Jónasson.**

Cornell Woolrich, ***The Bride Wore Black.*** The first suspense novel by one of the greatest of all noir authors opens with a bride and her new husband walking out of the church. A car speeds by, shots ring out, and he falls dead at her feet. Determined to avenge his death, she tracks down everyone in the car, concluding with a shocking surprise. It was filmed by Francois Truffaut in 1968, starring Jeanne Moreau. **Introduction by Eddie Muller.**

Cornell Woolrich, ***Deadline at Dawn.*** Quinn is overcome with guilt about having robbed a stranger's home. He meets Bricky, a dime-a-dance girl, and they fall for each other. When they return to the crime scene, they discover a dead body. Knowing Quinn will be accused of the crime, they race to find the true killer before he's arrested. A 1946 film starring Susan Hayward was loosely based on the plot. **Introduction by David Gordon.**

Cornell Woolrich, ***Waltz into Darkness.*** A New Orleans businessman successfully courts a woman through the mail but he is shocked to find when she arrives that she is not the plain brunette whose picture he'd received but a radiant blond beauty. She soon absconds with his fortune. Wracked with disappointment and loneliness, he vows to track her down. When he finds her, the real nightmare begins. **Introduction by Wallace Stroby.**